IT
ONLY
LOOKS
EASY

IT ONLY LOOKS EASY

Pamela
Curtis Swallow

 ROARING BROOK PRESS • BROOKFIELD, CONNECTICUT

Published by Roaring Brook Press
A Division of The Millbrook Press
2 Old New Milford Road
Brookfield, Connecticut 06804

LIBRARY OF CONGRESS CATALOGING-IN-PUBLICATION DATA

Swallow, Pamela Curtis.
    It only looks easy / Pamela Curtis Swallow.
    p. cm.
Summary: On the first day of seventh grade when Kat "borrows" a bicycle
to go see her dog who was hit the day before by a woman with Alzheimer's
disease, she learns about the serious consequences of impetuous actions
and manages to make some new friends in the process.
    [1. Interpersonal relations—Fiction. 2. Schools—Fiction. 3. Conduct
of life—Fiction. 4. Alzheimer's disease—Fiction.] I. Title.
    PZ7.S969895 It 2003
    [Fic]—dc21
                                    2002006611

ISBN   0-7613-1790-2 (trade edition)
10 9 8 7 6 5 4 3 2

ISBN   0-7613-2866-1 (library binding)
10 9 8 7 6 5 4 3 2 1

Book design by BTDnyc
Printed in the United States of America
First edition

FOR MY FAVORITE FISHERMAN, BILL,
AND IN MEMORY OF BEEZER, WHO LOVED CHEESE

Acknowledgments

FOR THEIR YEARS OF FRIENDSHIP and wisdom, I would like to express my gratitude to the RiverStone and Garden State writers: Pat Brisson, Denise Brunkus, Dorothy Carey, Nancy Cooney, Paula De Paolo, Joan Elste, Judy Freeman, Sally Keehn, Joyce McDonald, Trinka Hakes Noble, Margie Palatini, Wendy Pfeffer, Penny Pollock, Shirley Roffman, Virginia Troeger, Laura Whipple, Elvira Woodruff.

And special thanks to Sam Occhipinti, VMD; to math maven Gerard Dalton; to my daughters, Devin and Corrie; and to my editor, Deborah Brodie.

1

CHEDDAR IS ACTING AS WARDROBE consultant, lying under my bed with her tail sticking out. The tail lets me know that she's listening.

"Cheddar, the first day is important. Maybe I'll go with the blue skirt and striped top." *Thump.* "Or, maybe . . ." I dig through my bureau drawers, searching for the sweater I bought last week. "Maybe I could wear jeans and my new blue cotton sweater, if I can ever find it. What do you think?" *Thump, thump.* For ten years, Cheddar has been my trusted friend and advisor. Her opinion counts.

It's hot and humid. My window is open, and I can hear the kids across the street playing outside, shouting and arguing, making the most of the last day of summer vacation.

Thirsty and a little hungry, I go downstairs to the kitchen and check the fridge. The snack choices are pitiful. I take out a slice of cheese and begin to pull off the plastic wrap. Immediately, I hear Cheddar scrambling out from under my bed and hustling down the stairs. She can detect a slice of cheese two flights up.

Skidding around the corner, Cheddar stops short and sits in front of me. Her chubby golden body quivers. Her feathery retriever tail sweeps like a windshield wiper across the linoleum floor.

I tear off the corners of a slice and drop them into her mouth. They disappear without a chew. She looks toward the refrigerator, then back at me. "One more, but that's it."

I hear my sister, Hannah, laughing on the telephone in the family room. I look in and see her lying on the couch in front of the TV. She has the phone in one hand and the remote control in the other. She's wearing my new sweater. I sit down hard in the corduroy chair and glare at her. Cheddar sits by my feet, staring at the last piece of cheese.

"What? I'm on the phone, Kat," Hannah says.

I point to the sweater. "That's mine!"

With a raised index finger, Hannah gives her "just a minute" signal and continues her phone conversation. "High school is *huuuuge*. I have no idea where my homeroom is, so I'm getting there by seven-fifteen, just in case."

I sit there, running my finger along the grooves in the arm of the chair, getting more annoyed by the second. "That's my new sweater," I interrupt. "Take it off. I haven't even had a chance to wear it."

"Hold on, Amber," Hannah says. She gives me her blank, innocent expression, and then looks at the sweater as if only just noticing it. "This is yours? Are you sure? Hmmm. I'll be off the phone in a minute."

"Take it off *now*," I insist. "Right *now*."

Hannah uses the "just a minute" signal again. "Kat's being a pain," she says to her friend, and turns away from me.

I am about to yank my sweater off Hannah, when Cheddar gets up, ambles over to the couch, and steps on the cradle of the phone, disconnecting the call. She stands there, while the dial tone hums, then she walks slowly to the back door to be let outside.

"Ch-e-d-d-d-a-r," Hannah groans in frustration. "Jeez, watch where you're walking, would you?" She sighs loudly. "If you ask me, I'd say Cheddar doesn't see all that well anymore."

I let Cheddar out into the fenced-in yard. Before the subject of the sweater can come up again, Hannah quickly asks, "So, Kat, are you excited about tomorrow? Seventh grade's a really fun year. One of the best years of your life. You'll have a great time."

Not letting Hannah distract me from what she's wearing, I say, "I was saving that sweater for the first day of school. Why'd you take it?"

Casually Hannah combs her fingers through her thick, blond, perfect hair and then lets it fall to her shoulders. "I turned the air conditioner on. Then I needed a sweater. This was handy." She doesn't sound the least bit sorry.

"Handy? It was upstairs in my bottom drawer," I point out. "*Handy* is like when it's lying right here on the couch near you, and you just have to reach over and pick it up. You were in my room checking out my clothes."

Hannah shrugs. "It's not like I never loan *you* anything."

"You're supposed to ask first," I remind her.

There's a sudden commotion outside. I go to the window. I hear a car horn honking and kids' voices yelling, "No! Go away! Go home!"

"What's going on out there?" Hannah asks.

"It's Elspeth and Winston. They've been yelling all afternoon."

"Get *away*," Elspeth orders. "Shooo!"

"They must be talking to an animal or something," I say.

The honking starts up again. "What's with the car horn?" I open the front door and walk onto the lawn. I see the kids inside their mother's van, looking out and yelling through the nearly closed windows. And there's Cheddar on her hind legs, with her front paws on the van door, looking in.

She's supposed to be in our backyard. How'd she get over there? "Cheddar!" I call, "Come here!" She looks back at me over her shoulder. Then she looks at the kids.

"*Cheddar! Come here now!*" Finally, she gets down and slowly walks back across the street toward me. At the same time, a car turns the corner.

"*Cheddar!*" I scream.

2

ON THE FLOOR IN MY ROOM,
I lean against my bed, staring straight ahead. It's as if the wall is a movie screen and, over and over again, I keep seeing Cheddar walk across the street toward me—all because I called her.

I see the car coming at her. I yell for her to go back, to watch out, but there's no time. There's a thud, and she yelps. I run to her. Her eyes are open and she's breathing, but she isn't getting up. I scream for Hannah. She races to phone Mom and Dad. Then she brings a blanket to cover Cheddar.

I won't leave Cheddar. I don't hear or see what else is going on, I just kneel by Cheddar and talk to her. I stroke her head and tell her how sorry I am, how she will be all right, and how we'll take her to Dr. Goldstein and he'll help her. I whisper to her to please, please, be all right. All the way to the veterinary hospital, in the back of Mom's car, I stroke her and beg her to live.

Cheddar is with Dr. Goldstein now. We're all waiting. Dr. Goldstein told us that it could be a while. He has a lot to do for Cheddar and must work quickly. She's in shock. He's treating her for that and checking for internal injuries. X-rays, blood sample, tests, monitoring breathing, IV tubes, and I can't remember what else. I pleaded to stay with Cheddar, but Dr. Goldstein told us that it would be better if we wait at home. I hate that. What he didn't say scares me more than what he did say. The waiting is a nightmare.

∽⊚∿

No one talks at dinner. Most of the food goes into the garbage. That would never happen with Cheddar home.

Dad goes out to the backyard to see how Cheddar could have gotten out. When he comes in, he says that she dug under the fence. She's pretty big, so she had to have been working on the hole for a while. Probably ever since the Rooneys got their fancy new barbecue and started cooking outside every night. None of us can stand to think that we should have checked the fence regularly to see if she was planning to visit the neighbors. It's hard enough for me to know that she was coming to me when she was hit.

There has to be news soon. I lie on my bed listening for the phone. My best friend, Abby, calls and I tell her what happened. She tries to make me feel better, but can't. When she asks me who hit Cheddar, I tell her I don't even know. Some woman. I didn't pay attention.

It's ten o'clock when Mom and Dad come into my room; I'm lying in the dark with my arms across my forehead. They sit down on my bed. Mom's eyes are red. We don't say much. Mom pats my shoulder and Dad pats Mom's.

The ticking of the grandfather clock in the hall sounds loud. Usually, when I'm falling asleep, I hear Cheddar breathing under my bed. Sometimes she sighs or jingles her tags when she changes position. Tonight, only the clock.

In the morning, I wake up scared, more scared than I ever remember feeling. I hardly slept, and when I did, I had awful dreams. Images of the car veering toward Cheddar. Of her being knocked down. Of her lying on the road.

I go downstairs to the kitchen. "Mom? Did Dr. Goldstein call?"

She shakes her head. "Sorry, no. But we'll hear something soon, I'm sure."

Mom's already dressed. She looks as if she's actually going to work today. Pointing to the clock over the sink, she says, "Hannah's out of the shower. You have to get going."

I stare at her, surprised. "Mom, there's no way. I can't handle school."

"Please don't argue about this, Kat." She rubs her forehead and turns away.

Shuffling down the hall toward the bathroom, I see Dad sitting in his pajama bottoms and T-shirt, barefoot, in front of his computer. He writes for a news magazine and is usually up early, trying to make a deadline. Tufts of his graying hair stand up on top of his head.

"Dad, I *have* to stay home today. I have to wait for the phone call from Dr. Goldstein. I didn't get much sleep, and all I'll do at school is worry about Cheddar."

Dad sets down his mug of coffee and turns in his chair. "You need a hug," he says, taking off his reading glasses and holding out his arms.

I walk closer and lean against him, as he puts his arm around my waist. "Dad, I mean it. I can't deal with school today."

He nods. "I understand. But you won't gain anything by staying here. The waiting will be even harder. If we hear anything, we'll call you at school. As a matter of fact, we can try the animal hospital right now."

I hold my breath as Dad dials. He listens for a moment. "They have a machine on. They must not take calls until later."

I want to scream. He squeezes my hand. "Patience."

I can't relate to that word right now.

In the kitchen, I pick up a loaf of oatmeal bread to make toast. Mom is at the sink, shaking green tea leaves into the compost pail and rinsing her brown clay teapot.

"Mom?"

"Hmmm?" she answers, setting the teapot in the dish drain.

I try again. "*Please.*"

Mom sighs. "Kat, I know you're having a rough time. We all are."

I know the rest of what she'll say. It's no use. "Okay, I'll go, but it'll be a waste." I open the bag of bread, hold a slice in my hand, then put it back. There is no way that dry piece of bread is going down my tight throat.

Mom checks her watch. "You're going to be late if you don't start moving double time."

With the water turned up as hard as it can go, I stand in the shower and stare at the tile wall. So this is how one of the best years of my life begins? I should have figured that something bad was going to happen when Hannah said how great my year would be. In books, when you read something like, "everything is great," you just know that something terrible is about to happen. But in real life, you can miss the warnings. And then, *wham, slam,* sneak attack. Everything skids out of control.

3

MOM DROPS ME OFF IN FRONT OF the school and I go find my homeroom. Grace Fuhrman, with a new short, blunt haircut and with a price tag hanging off the back of her skirt, is holding up four new book covers. We haven't gotten our books yet, but she's ready. "Like these book covers?"

Even in the best of times, book covers don't excite me. I usually scrounge around the house for any sort of paper and end up covering my books with brown grocery bags.

Abby leans her long, thin body into the room and motions. I get up and go out into the hall. "Did you hear anything?" she asks. She twists a curl of red hair and waits.

I shake my head. "My dad called the veterinary hospital this morning. All he got was an answering machine."

The bell rings and Abby hurries to her homeroom, calling over her shoulder that she'll see me at lunch.

After first period, I see Matthew Mease, wearing a bright orange T-shirt, weaving through the crowd toward me from the other end of the hall. "Hey, I heard what happened to Cheddar," he says, looking worried. "Abby told me. I'm real sorry. Hope she's okay." Matthew lives just one street away from me. He loves dogs and takes care of Cheddar when we go away to places where we can't take her.

"I can't stand this waiting, Matt."

"Call the animal hospital again," he suggests.

"I'm going to, but someone's always on the pay phone. At lunchtime I'll be able to wait for it."

It feels like forever until lunch. Teachers are talking and moving in slow motion. I want to yell, "Will you *please* hurry up and finish?" Great back-to-school attitude. Finally, the bell at the end of fifth period rings, and I hurry to the pay phone outside the office.

Dennis Boyle is already there, arguing with someone about meeting after school. I pace back and forth, nervous and frustrated. I make sure Dennis sees that I need to make a call, and sigh loudly when he turns his back to ignore me. His baggy jeans hang low and the cuffs at his heels are dirty.

At last Dennis hangs up and *rattle-thwacks* open the phone booth door. It's amazing that the door doesn't come off its hinges and smash on the floor. Dennis grunts about someone being a jerk and marches off. Even after he turns the corner, I hear the chain that dangles off his pants jingling like a bad wind chime.

At last the phone is mine. I get the animal hospital's

number from the phone book hanging in the booth and I dial. I hold my breath. On the fourth ring, the receptionist answers. I ask her about Cheddar. She puts me on hold. I pray. She gets back on and says that Dr. Goldstein will call our house when he gets a chance. I sag against the wall, holding my fist to my mouth to keep from crying. What if Dad goes out and no one's there to get the call?

I find Abby and Matthew in the cafeteria and sit without talking for a few minutes. My cheese sandwich feels dry and heavy. The apple juice I'm swallowing barely helps.

Suddenly I stand up. "I'm going there."

"Now? To the vet's? During *school?*" Abby asks.

I pick up my juice container and lunch bag. "Yup. I can't take this waiting. I'm leaving."

"How are you getting there?" Matthew asks.

"I'll manage." I march back to the pay phone, dial information, and call for a taxi.

"Both cabs are out right now." The voice belongs to a bored-sounding woman. "I can radio and have one come pick you up in a while."

In a while isn't good enough.

"Should be there in about twenty, twenty-five minutes or so," she adds.

"Never mind. That's okay." I've seen the two taxi drivers moseying around town, never in a hurry. I can't wait for the slow-motion cab company. Besides, I might not even have enough money with me to pay for a taxi.

I get my backpack from my locker and walk toward the gym door. If I'm going to cut school on the very first day, I shouldn't announce it by marching big as life right past the main office. As I'm about to go out the door, I see my gym teacher, Ms. Cohen, striding toward me. The whistle around her neck bounces from one side of her chest to the other. I pretend to be getting a drink from the water fountain. When I look up, she's gone. I slip outside.

Standing by the back of the gym, I can hear balls bouncing against the inside wall. I think about walking to the animal hospital, but that could take forever.

The bike rack catches my eye. I could get to the hospital a lot faster on a bike. Too bad I decided over the summer that, as a seventh grader, I'm not going to ride to school anymore, or I'd have my bike right there. But there is one bike with no lock. It would be easy to borrow it. I look at it for a moment, noticing an *I* ❤ *NY* sticker, held in place on the handlebar with candy-cane-striped reflector tape. I hesitate; then I pull my assignment pad out of my backpack and scribble:

> **To the owner of the blue Schwinn**
> **with the red hand grips (and no lock):**
> **Emergency — I had to borrow your bike.**
> **Sorry. I'll bring it back tomorrow.**
> **I'll even give you a lock.**
> **Promise.**

I don't sign my name to the note that I can hardly believe I just wrote. I don't want to be tracked down and stopped from doing what I have to do. I push down my sock and pull off the Band-Aid on my heel. It's the only thing I can find to stick the note to the rack.

As I ride away, I think about the kind of trouble I could be in if the bike's owner doesn't accept my borrowing plan. My fingerprints are probably all over the bike rack and the Band-Aid. The police could be at my door by suppertime.

Our town is sprawling. It's not a tidy package, with important buildings neatly placed together. Things are pretty far apart. When I get to Elm Street, I ask the gas station attendant if there are any shortcuts to the veterinary hospital. He tells me a way that will take only fifteen minutes if I can keep the directions straight. It takes me longer.

I pull into the parking area and lean the bike against the side of the building. I look around for Mom's Explorer and Dad's Toyota. Bumping into either, or both, of them would add the topping to the giant heap of trouble I am probably already in.

I can feel my stomach tensing as I reach for the door. Before I pull the handle, the door opens and an older couple walks out. Both of them have gray hair and look about my grandparents' age. The woman seems worried and uncertain as she holds her brown leather purse with one hand and the man's arm with the other. He speaks to her quietly. "We'll call again this evening and see what we can learn." I feel sorry for them. They must have a pet in the animal hospital, and I know how that feels.

Looking at me, the woman says, "Hello." She twists the strap of her purse. "Do you work here?"

I wasn't expecting that question. "No, I don't."

She smiles. "Well, you look as if you might. I thought you might know something."

"No. I'm just here to find out about my dog," I answer.

"That is a coincidence, isn't it, David? We came to . . ." her voice trails off.

He puts his hand over hers and gently moves toward the parking lot. "We are here to inquire, Ann." He smiles at me. "Good-bye."

The reception area is pretty full. There are five people holding either cats or dogs and two people without pets. The woman behind the desk is frazzled. She's printing bills, checking records, answering the phone, calling people in to see Dr. Goldstein, and sighing a lot.

I step up to the counter in front of her and wait. Eventually she looks over her glasses at me. "Yes? May I help you?"

"I'm Kat Randall and my dog Cheddar is back there." I point behind her. "She was in an accident yesterday and I need to know how she is. I want to see her. I *have* to."

"They're very, *very* busy today." She emphasized *very*. "Didn't someone tell you that they'll call when they have a chance?" she asks.

"Have a *chance?* Do they, do *you*, know what the waiting is like? I don't think anyone's even home to get Dr. Goldstein's call. That's my dog and I have to know how she is. I need to see her." I can feel tears welling up in my eyes. I stand there, not budging.

She sighs and says, "Please have a seat." Then she pauses and adds, "No school this afternoon?" I pretend not to hear. Where I'm supposed to be is not her problem.

The room smells like pets and disinfectant. I don't even try to read while I wait, knowing it would be useless. I look at the people and their pets. There's a spaniel with weepy eyes, sitting on the lap of an old man. He strokes the dog's fur and talks to it softly. I think about moving near them so I can stroke the dog, too. Across from him is a thin woman with a gray cat in a carrying case. The cat is crying. A large Doberman comes in, toenails clicking and scratching on the tile floor. The small young woman on the other end of the leash is having a hard time keeping him close to her.

It feels as if no one remembers that I'm waiting. I sit and sit. Pets and owners come and go. It's almost three o'clock when Dr. Goldstein comes to the waiting room door and motions to me to come with him. We step into the back hall and he says, "Kat, I know you're anxious to know how Cheddar is." He pauses. "You're here by yourself?"

"Yes."

"Well, I don't have all the answers yet, but here's what I know. Her back right leg is broken." I cringe to hear that. "I'm not sure if she'll need surgery for that. I've asked a colleague of mine who's a specialist in orthopedics to stop in and assist me in evaluating the damage to the bone. One thing for sure—she is terribly sore all over."

He takes off his glasses and wipes them on his lab coat. I know that there's more. I wait.

"It's what may be going on internally that we can't see, that I'm not totally sure about yet," he says. "X-rays are helpful, but don't always show everything. She doesn't appear to be bleeding internally, which is good. So I'm hoping everything is okay."

"When will you know?" I ask.

"Before much longer." He puts his hand on my shoulder. "You understand that with an older dog, we don't expect the same kind of recovery. It can take longer. Sometimes there are internal injuries and—"

I know what's coming and I interrupt. "But she *could* be all right, couldn't she? She could have a broken leg and lots of aches, and that's all. And then she could get better, right?"

"Yes, that could happen," he says.

"Can I see her?" I ask.

"You may, but understand that she won't be acting like her regular self. She has a couple of tubes attached—an IV for shock and a catheter."

I'm not really sure what all that means, but I nod. We go into a part of the animal hospital that I've never seen, beyond the regular examination rooms, to an area where they do surgery and treat serious problems. Cheddar is lying on her left side in a cage. She has a tube, held in place with tape, in her right front leg; the tube is attached to a bottle hanging above her. She has another tube coming from between her back legs. Dr. Goldstein opens the door to the cage, so that I can stroke Cheddar and talk to her. I put my face to her ear and whisper that I'm here and that she'll be all right. I tell her that she'll be home soon. I say that I love her. I tell her I'm so sorry. She looks at me. I know she understands.

"Does she get painkillers?" I ask.

"An aspirin-like substance," he says.

"That doesn't seem like much," I comment.

"It helps."

I have a hard time leaving Cheddar. Dr. Goldstein takes my arm and walks me to the hall. He tells me that later on, before he leaves the clinic for the day, he'll let us know what he thinks. He tells me he understands how I'm feeling. He also grew up with a dog who was a part of the family. He gives me a hug and tells me to stay positive.

I'm trying not to cry. I want so much to run back to Cheddar. I walk to where I left the bike against the side of the building. I take a deep breath and think about how Dr. Goldstein had said to stay positive. How he said that Cheddar could recover.

Tomorrow morning I'll get to school early, leave the bike with a nice lock, and maybe even a flower or something, and that will be that. I stop short when I get to where I'd left the bike leaning against the building.

The bike is gone.

4

IT CAN'T BE. THE BIKE HAS TO BE where I left it. Maybe I turned the wrong way going out the door and I'm looking at the wrong side of the building. Trying to stay calm, I walk around the whole outside of the hospital, checking each wall. No bike.

Unbelievable! The bike I borrowed is now stolen. Maybe it isn't actually stolen. Someone could have just moved it, for safekeeping. With that bit of hope, I go back inside.

The receptionist looks over her glasses. I tell her that my bike is missing. I ask if anyone has said anything to her about a bike. She shakes her head.

I walk around outside again, just in case the bike has suddenly reappeared. It hasn't.

What a mess. The kind of mess that can't exactly remain a secret. I'll have to find the person whose bike I took and explain what happened, even though I don't know what happened myself.

Since I'm going to have to confess anyway, I decide to call home from the pay phone and see if Dad can pick me up.

With the help of call-waiting, I get through to Hannah. She says that Dad went to drop off his news article and to meet with his editor. She doesn't know when he'll be back. Mom won't be home before six o'clock. I don't tell Hannah where I am. After one last futile search for the bike, I start walking.

※

Nearly an hour later, I walk into the house and drop my backpack by the door. Hannah's voice carries from the family room. "Yes! And he's in my homeroom!" A moment later she says, "Just a minute, Amber. Hey, Kat, where have you been?"

"I went to the veterinary hospital to see Cheddar." I kick off my sneakers and flop in the corduroy chair.

"You did? *That's* where you were when you called? Tell me about Cheddar. How is she?" Hannah asks.

"Dr. Goldstein says that she has a broken hind leg, and maybe more things wrong."

"Gotta go, Amber. Talk to you later." Hannah hangs up quickly and takes a deep breath. "Oh, no. What else?"

"Dr. Goldstein isn't sure yet. It could be only the leg and lots of bruises. Or there could be internal problems. He's going to call later."

"Internal problems? That could be bad," she says softly. She's quiet for a moment. "I mean, what do they do about that?"

"I don't know." I can't keep straight what he said. We sit silently for a while, both afraid to get very far into the subject of Cheddar's injuries.

Finally Hannah says, "You know what I can't stop thinking about, Kat? That time I was out back with Cheddar, throwing her tennis ball, and I accidentally hit her smack in the eye with it. I will never forget the way she looked, blinking her watery, hurt eye and trying to smile that silly crooked smile of hers as she came to me and sat in my lap. She was so forgiving."

"I remember that. I feel bad about every sad thing that's ever happened to Cheddar."

We're quiet for a while longer. Then Hannah asks, "So, how'd you get to Dr. Goldstein's anyway? When did you leave school? Don't tell me that you left school *early* to go." Her mouth is wide open.

"Yup."

Hannah is speechless for a rare moment. Finally she says, "Really? You left school *early*? I wouldn't have the nerve."

"I had to do it. I couldn't take the waiting." I tell her how I walked out, took a bike, rode to the animal hospital. I tell her about finally being able to see Cheddar and talk to Dr. Goldstein. Then I tell her about the missing bike.

She's stunned. "*Nooo!* No way! You're kidding."

"I wish." I yank a loose blue thread off the sleeve of my sweater, ball it up, and tweak it into the air. "I think I'm going to have to buy a new bike for some unsuspecting kid. What does a decent bike cost, anyway?"

Hannah shrugs. "Don't know. I guess you'll have to go to a bike shop and look at ones like the one you lost." She looks at me sympathetically. "I have a feeling that decent bikes cost a lot."

"The one I borrowed was pretty good, I guess." We go to my room so I can look at my savings account book. The $73.22 balance isn't going to get a replacement bike. Barely a tire and a bell. "I'm going to have to earn a heap of extra money, baby-sitting the best years of my life away. If you get called to sit, and you don't feel like doing it, let me take the jobs, okay? You already said you don't like sitting for the Staffords, right? Not after that incident with Winston and the Alka-Seltzer tablet in his mouth, when he made you believe he had rabies. I'll take Stafford jobs."

Hannah shrugs. "Fine. Winston's horrible."

"Want to buy that bracelet of mine that you're wearing?" I ask. "Six-fifty."

"No, thanks," she says, slipping it off, dropping it onto my bed, and changing the subject. "Are you going to tell Mom and Dad right away?"

I nod. "I'm scared, but it's better to get it over with, before they find out some other way."

"I think they'll understand. It's not as if you have a theft record or as if this is part of a crime spree. You were thinking about Cheddar."

I hope she's right about Mom and Dad understanding. "And what kind of trouble do you think I'm in for cutting school? Teachers look at the absence list and check who's missing, don't they?"

"Well, some do. You could probably just say you felt sick and had to go home. Most teachers accept that, from kids who have a good reputation, anyway."

"It's too early in the year to have *any* reputation," I comment. Then I realize I'll have quite a name for myself very soon. In fact several: bike thief, school skipper, busted.

"Mine ought to help," Hannah says, matter-of-factly. She's right, although teachers who expect a younger version of perfect Hannah learn soon enough that they're not getting one.

Probably trying to get my mind on something else besides Cheddar and all the trouble I'm in, Hannah says, "I think it's time to grow your hair. It would look good."

I tuck a short strand of brown hair behind my ear. "I'm not good with hair. Less is better. But I wouldn't mind *out*growing my freckles. Do you think there are fewer than there used to be?"

Hannah leans closer to look. "Maybe. But anyway, they're cute with your face."

I wonder if she'd think they were cute on her flawless face. I could learn a lot from Hannah about how to be practically perfect, but this is not the time. I think about asking her if high school is hard, but I realize I'd be asking the wrong person. Hannah never worries about her work; she just does it, usually at the last minute, and impresses everyone.

We're silent again. Hannah rubs her forehead and looks down at the floor. I sigh loudly and stare up at the ceiling.

"Kat, this is a terrible start to the year. But I honestly think that our stubborn, comical old character of a dog will get better. And I think that eventually the bike thing will blow over. Things won't stay this bad." It would be nice if she's right, but I wonder.

Every time the phone rings, I jump. It's almost six-fifteen when Dr. Goldstein calls. We all stand by the phone while Mom talks to him. She reaches for a pencil and paper and writes a few things down:

> **Fracture—back leg**
>
> **Orthopedist tomorrow**
>
> **Fluids**
>
> **Heart strong**
>
> **No sign—bleeding**

I hold my hands in a prayer position. I glance at Hannah. She's doing the same thing.

When Mom is through talking to Dr. Goldstein, we wait. She takes a deep breath, and picks up the piece of paper with her notes. "All right. This is what he said. Cheddar's back right leg is fractured and might need pins. We won't know until the orthopedist looks at her. At any rate, no surgery can be done until Dr. Goldstein is sure that she's stable and gaining strength. He's been monitoring her closely. Her eyes look good, and her breathing is getting stronger. He said that, from the X-rays and from blood tests that were done, it looks as if there isn't any internal bleeding. And her membrane color is normal, which indicates that her circulation is good. All that is positive."

Dad asks, "So, is he optimistic?"

"More so now than when we brought her in and she was in shock. He's been able to keep her pressure up with a steroid IV drip. And her neurological signs are good."

"So, now what?" Hannah asks. "Can't he tell us if she'll be all right?"

"He's hopeful, Hannah. But it's still a bit early to know," Mom answers.

We're all wrung out. We hug each other and try to give reassuring looks. What we all want is to have Cheddar back home with us. I hate that she's in a cage, lying still, attached to tubes. Home, I could sleep next to her. I could give her love, encouragement, and cheese.

Dad clears his throat. "I say that we all concentrate very hard and send Cheddar positive energy. There have been many studies showing what amazing power it can have. That, along with a great vet, could be the winning combination we need for Team Cheddar."

I feel better. But then I remember the bike issue, still not dealt with. I cringe when the phone rings, imagining what a conference call among my parents, the principal, and the police might be like.

It's Abby calling to say that she's told a lot of people that I felt sick in school, so maybe teachers would get the idea that I had a medical excuse for leaving early. We talk about Cheddar and I tell her what Dr. Goldstein said. Upstairs in my room, where Mom and Dad can't hear, I tell her about the bike. "That is the *worst* luck," she says. "I'll let you have what I earn taking care of the Foleys' cat while they're away."

"No way, Abby. You don't have to do that."

"Taking care of little Puff isn't like real work. Cat sitting is easy. So the money earned isn't like real hard-earned money. Case closed." No wonder Abby and I have been friends for so long.

I struggle during dinner, trying to decide just when to tell Mom and Dad about the bike.

The conversation is mostly about the person who ran her car into Cheddar. Mom had spoken with her quickly before we left for the veterinary hospital.

"It seems that the woman may have glanced away from the road to look for something in her car. She was very confused about what happened," Mom explains.

"Was she drinking or anything?" Hannah asks.

Mom shakes her head. "The police said that it didn't seem so. But they did say that she was not sure where she was or what had occurred. She was extremely disoriented, confused, and upset. The police drove her home."

"Do you even know who she is?" I ask.

"Her name must have come up. Lewis, Lanman, Lombard . . . I don't know, can't remember. Something like that. My mind was on Cheddar," Mom answers.

Then Dad asks about school. I tell what I can, which is only about my morning; no one notices that I left out the second half of the school day. Hannah has plenty to say about her first day as a freshman.

"Dori got her necklace stuck in her braces. And Amber got glasses—just plain glass, no prescription, just as an accessory. And at lunch Samuel made believe he couldn't speak English, and the cafeteria ladies thought he was a foreign exchange student."

Dad pushes back his chair and begins to clear the table. "Well, who's helping with dishes?"

Hannah offers, "I'll do them." It isn't her turn. Either her kind streak is kicking in, or else she realizes that she has my necklace on and I can bring that up in front of Mom and Dad. They aren't big on people taking other people's things without asking. Wait till they find out what I took.

"Mom, Dad," I say, as they are leaving the table, "I've got something to tell you."

5

AS I BEGIN TELLING THEM THAT
I left school early and took a bike from the school bike rack,
I can see from their faces, and know from their stony
response, that they think it's pretty serious. And that's *before*
I tell them about the bike really being stolen. When I get to
that part, Mom shakes her head. "Oh, Kat. I can't believe
this."

"This is serious, Katia," Dad says, as I knew he would.

"Very serious," Mom adds.

But they stay calm, at least on the outside. We talk about
the mistakes I made that afternoon. They say they understand how much I'd wanted to get to the animal hospital, but
they think I used terrible judgment.

We decide that since I don't know whose bike I lost, and
don't know the serial number or proper identification of the
bike, I have to wait until tomorrow to talk to the owner and
to the police. Then, if the bike isn't found in a few days, I'll
have to make arrangements to replace it.

"It'll take me a long time to earn enough money for a bike."

"That's right," Mom says. "And it won't be fair to keep the bike owner waiting while you save. We'll have to lend you the money for the bike. You'll then have to pay us back, as promptly as possible. You are *not* to drag this out."

"We could start with no allowance," I suggest.

"Right," Dad agrees. "And you'll have to actively seek jobs, as well. We'll leave that for you to work out."

Their disappointment in me is obvious. All I can do about that now is try to fix things as best I can, but that will have to begin tomorrow.

Hannah pokes her head in. "Mom, Dad, there are two messages on our answering machine from a Mr. David Lawrence. Do we know him?"

"Don't think so," Mom replies. "Maybe he just wants to sell us something."

"He said he'd call back," Hannah says.

Lying in bed, I think of Cheddar. I'd give anything right now to hear her breathing and thumping her tail in her sleep. It doesn't seem possible that in such a short time so much has changed. I want to be able to go back and fix what happened. I want to go across the street and get Cheddar and walk her safely home. As if she's close and can hear me, I whisper, "I'm so sorry, Cheddar. You're going to be all right. Please heal and come home. We need each other. At least, I sure need you. Things are going horribly."

◦◦◦

In the morning, there's the matter of the missing bike and its owner. I'm up early, dressed and ready to leave, before Hannah's done with her marathon shower.

"Are you going early to wait for the owner of the bike?" Mom asks.

"Yes." For the second day in a row, I dread going to school. All during my walk there, I want to turn around and go somewhere else.

The school yard and bike rack are empty when I get there. I stand where I can watch the bike rack and the front of the building at the same time. Pretty soon buses and parents begin dropping kids off. Maybe I should be wearing a *Guilty Bike Borrower* sign around my neck to make it easier for the bike owner to identify me.

As I stand watching the cars pull up front, I notice that a lot of people look like their cars. Car salespeople must try to match people and cars that way. Dennis Boyle, with slicked, dark hair, gets out of a sleek, black Mustang with a racing stripe. Small, round, blond Marsha Cushing and her similar-looking mother drive up in a beige minivan. Mrs. Allen's nose matches the front of the Volkswagen Beetle she parks.

Glancing toward the bike rack, I can see that kids are

starting to arrive, but so far no one is bikeless. I walk over to wait. Trying to look casual, I pull a book out of my backpack and flip through it, as I lean against the end of the bike rack. Out of the corner of my eye, I see a girl and a woman walking toward me. The woman is wearing a gray blazer with black pants. Her straight brown hair is pulled tightly back. The girl has pale skin and shoulder-length hair the same color as a gerbil I once had. Her green jumper hangs loose on her small, thin body. She must be either new or else a sixth grader. I don't know her.

I feel my hand shaking as I put the book away and look up. "Hi," I say, looking at the girl. "I'm Kat Randall. Was it your bike I borrowed yesterday?"

She nods and looks around. "Did you bring it back?"

The woman stares hard at me. I swallow before answering. "Well, that was my plan. I meant to have it here this morning, but this is what happened, from the beginning: My dog was hit by a car the afternoon before school started and she's in the veterinary hospital. I wasn't able to get much news about her, and I couldn't stand the not knowing and the waiting."

"So to check on your dog, you took my daughter's bike?" the woman says. "Just helped yourself to it?"

I apologize. "I did leave a note, but it was still wrong to take the bike. I'm sorry."

"And where is the bike now?" the mother asks, scowling.

"Well, what happened was that I had to wait a long time before I finally got to talk with the veterinarian and see my dog. When I was leaving to go home, I went to get the bike. And the bike was gone." I have trouble looking at them.

"Gone?" the girl says.

"Stolen?" the mother says. "For a *second* time? I don't believe this. You're *sure* you looked everywhere?" She looks disgusted. Her mouth and eyes make the most unpleasant expression I've ever seen on a person who isn't a mean character in a fairy tale.

"I looked and looked. It wasn't anywhere at the animal hospital. We could call there now to see if it showed up," I suggest. The woman nods at me. "Obviously, we should do that. We should also notify the police. And we should speak to the principal of this school."

I bite my lip and look at the girl. She's looking at her mother. "Mom, please. Don't—"

"I'm so sorry about this," I say. "I'll do everything I can to get your bike back. And if it doesn't turn up soon, I'll pay for another one."

The girl says quietly, "I really liked that bike. I'd like my own back."

"My daughter got that bicycle for her birthday last spring," the woman states. "It was *not* cheap. She's been careful with it, except that yesterday she forgot her lock. And, of course, that had to be the day you came along. What kind of people go to this school anyway?"

That stung. Because of me, she has a bad impression of the whole school. "There's a phone by the side of the school," I say. "We can call now."

"I'll use my own phone," the girl's mother says, taking her cell phone from her pocketbook. I tell her the number of the animal hospital. The news isn't good. No bike. She calls the police department next and describes the bike in detail. I hear my name mentioned. Watching her as she speaks, I decide she looks like a headache. A walking, talking headache.

"There," she says, once the calls are made. "Now if the bike isn't recovered by the end of the weekend, you will need to replace it." We exchange names, addresses, and phone numbers. I learn that their last name is Whiezersky and that the girl is Melody. I offer to lend her my bike until she has one again, but Mrs. Whiezersky says that there has been enough use of other people's bicycles for one week, and that she'll drive Melody to school. "It's certainly inconvenient and is going to add extra pressure to our already hectic mornings," she makes a point of saying.

I wince, imagining what hectic mornings with Melody's mother must be like.

"One last question," Mrs. Whiezersky says. "How far from the school do you live?"

"About fifteen minutes, walking."

With an unpleasant, satisfied smirk, she says, "So you could have gone home and gotten your own bicycle. But instead, you simply chose to take someone else's."

I swallow hard. "I'm sorry. It was wrong. But I was hurrying. I didn't think—"

She holds up her hand and cuts me off. "That is correct." She punches the words out. "You didn't think."

The bell rings and Melody and I move toward the door. "Mom," Melody says, turning to face her mother, "please don't come to the office and talk to the principal. I don't want this to be a big thing at school."

Mrs. Whiezersky doesn't answer. Glancing at each other, Melody and I go inside, neither of us sure what Mrs. Whiezersky plans to do. I tell Melody again that I'm sorry, and then we head for our lockers. The school day hasn't even begun, and I'm exhausted.

Matthew stops me in the hall on the way to homeroom. "What's the news on Cheddar?"

I tell him what I know.

"That's good. Sounds like an improvement, don't you think?" Matthew says.

I also tell Matthew about my bike fiasco.

"Stolen bikes can be picked apart or repainted fast. They're hard to track down," he says. "But I'll help you look for it."

In homeroom, I remember I'm supposed to have covered my books. I look around the room, hoping to see something I can cover them with—a paper bag, newspaper, paper towels, anything. Nothing. I'll have to keep my books out of sight. Some teachers give detention for no book covers. And some students, such as Grace Fuhrman, are very interested in the book cover issue.

Most kids ignore the morning announcements in homeroom and socialize until the bell dismisses them for first period. Keith Damiano sits coolly tipped in his chair, trying to get Marsha Cushing's attention. He leans back with his right arm stretched behind him and his fingertips resting on Marsha's desk, while she sits sideways, talking to her best friend, Denise. With a sudden *bammm*, Keith's chair goes over backward. That gets Marsha's attention. But you can tell from the surprised look on Keith's face that it isn't what he had in mind. Trying to remain cool, he stretches and pretends to yawn as he lies on his back.

"Keith, are you okay?" asks Mr. Griff, our homeroom teacher, leaning forward and peering over his desk at Keith.

"I meant to do that," Keith says, his face red. The class claps as he slowly gets up.

Mr. Griff shakes his head and picks up his newspaper, mumbling, "One hundred and seventy-eight days to go."

≈≈≈

In science, Mr. Corento, who smells like a dentist, stands at the front of the room and talks about the experiment involving heat and light that he is about to do for the class. "Maybe he'll show us how to blow up the school," Dennis Boyle remarks, under his breath. "That would be a treat for our young minds." He snickers.

As Mr. Corento moves about the room in his lab coat, three greasy clumps of hair fall over his shiny forehead. I have an urge to dash up to him and snip them off, but it would be dumb to annoy him. He's going to be annoyed soon enough, when he realizes what a science zero I am.

I watch Mr. Corento take some bottles out of his lab closet. He looks ill at ease in front of the class. Hannah told me that last year a boy had hidden in that closet and made weird noises. When Mr. Corento opened the door, the boy danced out, singing, "Ninety-nine beakers of beer on the wall!"

Nerve. That's nerve. Stronger nerves than I've got right now. Every time a classroom door opens, or the loudspeaker starts to hum before an announcement begins, I jump, expecting to hear, *"Kat Randall—you're nailed."*

In the cafeteria at lunchtime, Abby says, "I've finally got my between-classes walking route worked out. It's brilliant."

"So how many times do you see 'Tim Terrific' on this fabulous route?" She did the same thing last year. Hers is a long-term crush.

"Eight. Counting this lunch period. I'm so excellent at this. Maybe I can start a business working out customized routes for people. What do you suppose kids would pay?"

"Not a lot. There's the mad-dash factor and the risk of detention. Not everyone wants to skid around corners and sprint down hallways on the complete opposite side of the school from where they need to be when the bell's about to ring, just to catch a glimpse of the boy or girl they like. It would be pretty dangerous if we all did it."

"That's all part of the thrill," Abby says.

"What thrill?" Tim asks, setting down his tray across from us and looking at Abby expectantly.

Abby's face turns red. "Nothing. What's up? How's your schedule working out?"

"Okay," he answers, not noticing Abby's red face. "How's yours?"

Matthew sets three cartons of milk and a bagel next to Tim's things. "Save this place for me, please. I'm going for ice cream."

I'm just pulling my sandwich out of its plastic bag when the loudspeaker blares, *"Katia Randall to the office. Katia Randall to the office."*

6

let on, I walk into the office. Mrs. Landes, the school secretary, looks at me with magnified eyes through her thick glasses. She has cracker crumbs stuck to the front of her fuzzy red sweater.

"I heard my name," I say.

"Yes, you have a call, Katia." She points to the phone by her desk.

"Do you know who it is?" I ask.

Mrs. Landes nods. "Your father." Then she gets up and walks over to the other side of the room, where Dennis Boyle is sitting outside the principal's office. "Mr. Boyle, you are *not* to dismantle that door hinge. Keep your hands in your lap." She marches back to her desk.

My hand is shaking as I reach for the phone. I take a deep breath. "Dad?"

"Kat, I didn't mean to scare you, but I wanted to let you know that Dr. Goldstein called with news that Cheddar is doing much better today. He says it's a positive sign."

I exhale. "That is so great, Dad. Phew! What exactly did he say?"

"He's been monitoring her closely and all vital signs are stronger now. If she continues to show progress and gain strength, the leg can be treated."

"Is she going to need surgery? Pins in her leg?"

"He and the orthopedic specialist looked at the X-rays together and decided that a cast would probably do the job."

"That's a relief. Do you know when she can come home?"

"Dr. Goldstein didn't say," Dad answers. "Why don't we stop in there later? Come straight home, and we'll go as soon as I get back from the library."

I feel so much better after the call. Everything else that I've been worrying about seems less of a huge deal. In my afternoon classes, things go all right. No one seems too concerned about where I was yesterday.

∽✅∽

Coming into the house and not being greeted by Cheddar is strange. She always meets us at the door.

Abby stops by to keep me company while I wait for Dad. We make a list of ways I can earn money for the bike. "Baby-sitting's probably the thing I'll do most. That, and raking leaves," I say.

"And don't forget," adds Abby, "I'm giving you the Puff-sitting money."

"Look, Abby, you don't have to do that. I got myself into

this mess. You had nothing to do with it. You should keep the money you earn."

"You'd do it for me, Kat." She changes the subject. "Hey, what do you think of the new math teacher?" She brushes clear nail polish on her short fingernails.

"Mr. Billings? Seems nice," I answer.

"Cute, too. I heard three girls say they have crushes on him." She blows on her nails.

"They may get over that. I think he's going to be a hard teacher. He said he doesn't want, and won't even *allow*, parents to help with homework. Students can work with each other, but parents are supposed to stay out of it. That's going to cause real problems for some people, like Grace Fuhrman. Her mom always helps her with her work."

"Yeah, no more mother-daughter homework assignments," Abby comments. "Her mom will have to concentrate on Grace's cheerleading. I've heard that she goes to all Grace's practices and competitions."

"That's *involved*," I say.

"Do you see how Grace flirts with Tim?" Abby says. "She's not even one bit subtle about it. It's so, *so-o-o* obvious. What if he notices her before he notices me? Wouldn't that be just great. I've spent the best years of my life"—she waves her index finger the way she always does when she's making an important point—"trying to help Tim realize that we were destined for each other." Abby sighs dramatically and flops backward on my bed with her hand across her brow. "I've fallen flat on my heart. Why can't he look at me as the woman of his dreams instead of the old pal he's known since kindergarten?"

"Give him time, Abby. Boys take longer to evolve." I smile at her and change the subject. "Do you think that if I haven't been called to the office by now for cutting school yesterday, it wasn't noticed?"

"I'd say you got away with it," Abby answers. She stands up, walks to the closet, and begins flipping through the clothes. "Hey, when are you going to bust out these new clothes, so I can start borrowing them?"

"You'll be lucky if my sneaky snatcher sister leaves any-thing for you but empty hangers."

Abby leans over and picks up my white earmuffs from the closet floor. "Remember the day you wore these last year because Dennis Boyle kept riding back and forth in front of the house chanting, 'Kat Randall is a bird-brain, a turd-brain.'"

"I was muffling his annoying voice. He was trying to tor-ment me because I wouldn't go to Keith's pool party with him," I say. "That was a whole year ago, and he *still* acts mad. And he still gets in trouble. I saw him sitting outside the principal's office today. What'd he do? Do you know?"

"He mouthed off at Ms. Cohen in gym. She made him change out of his baggy pants and wear loaners," Abby says. "He accused her of forcing him to look like a male ballerina."

We hear Dad pull into the driveway. Abby gets up and

pokes her feet back into her sandals. "Well, that about covers it, Kat. We've discussed the important issues, including your languishing wardrobe, which I'd very much like to get involved with. Gotta go now." She passes Dad on the stairs. "Hi, Mr. Randall. Bye, Mr. Randall."

~◊~

Cheddar raises her head and thumps her tail softly as I get close. It's one of the best moments ever. I put my cheek next to hers and stroke her, as Dr. Goldstein talks to us. We're all feeling a lot better about how she's doing. Tomorrow morning, as long as she keeps improving, Dr. Goldstein will put the cast on her leg. Then, when she's well enough, she'll come home. I can't wait.

7

I'M GLAD THAT THERE'S ONLY ONE more school day in this first, awful week of school. My goal is to get through Friday without incident.

I'm not expecting trouble in social studies. I'm sitting quietly, staring at Mr. Creston and watching the ball of spit on his bottom lip stretch when he speaks. "Most early humans were troglodytes," he says, drawing out the last word. "Trogggg-lo-dytes." I watch the spit, waiting to see whether it will divide into two smaller balls or snap back to one big one.

"A trogggg-lo-dyte was a cave dweller," Mr. Creston explains.

It's annoying the way Grace Fuhrman nods, as if she already knows what the word means and is agreeing with him. She isn't wasting any time getting on the good side of her teachers.

Mr. Creston turns to write *troglodyte* on the blackboard. The back of his chalk-smudged tweedy jacket reminds me of oatmeal with a splash of milk. "Copy this vocabulary word down. It also refers to hermits, people with primitive habits. Anthropoid apes, such as the chimpanzee, are also classified as trogggg-lo-dytes," Mr. Creston continues. "Any questions? Hmmmm?"

Grace's hand shoots up. Mr. Creston smiles and nods for her to speak. "Mr. Creston, shouldn't we all have our social studies textbook covered by now?" She stares right at mine.

Groans and assorted gestures from several members of the class follow. Dennis Boyle mumbles something about Grace keeping her snotty nose out of other people's business.

Mr. Creston sighs, looks down, and shakes his head. "That was not actually the sort of question I anticipated, but, yes, books should be covered." He glances at me and then at his seating chart. "Let's see . . . Ms. Randall. Hannah Randall's sister?" He looks reverently toward heaven at the mention of Hannah's name.

I nod.

"Hmmm . . . well, please get a cover on your book." His eyes scan the room. "Mr. Munez, Mr. Boyle, Mr. Mease—be sure that yours, too, are covered by our next class, or be prepared to stay for detention. School policy. Anyone else without a cover? Seems not. Well, then let's move on."

I scowl at Grace, the self-appointed seventh-grade snitch, and whisper, "Happy now?"

～⊙～

"Kat! Over here!" Abby calls across the cafeteria as I walk in. She waves her lunch bag. I slide onto the bench next to her.

Tim sets down his tray and mumbles something about wishing the school would get decent-sized furniture, as he bumps his long legs against the table and bench. "So, *ouch*, how's your dog doing?"

"Better," I say. "Thanks."

Keith sets his tray next to Tim's. "So, what's up with Mr. Corento? He's weird. All twitchy looking. It's tradition for seventh graders to prank him, you know." Keith grins and looks around. "Who's gonna do it first this year?"

Probably Dennis Boyle, I think to myself. It sure isn't going to be me. I don't need to push my luck in science.

Keith pokes Tim. "Check out Grace Fuhrman. She's over there across from Marsha," he says. Grace is kicking her legs and flapping her arms while eating a thin sandwich.

"Whoa, look at that," Tim says. "What the—"

"I bet I know," I say. "In homeroom I heard her telling people that she's going to model. That means she has to be skinny."

"So what's with the kicking and flapping action?" Matthew asks.

"Burning off calories," I explain. "Don't you guys know that if you keep moving while you're eating, calories don't count?"

The boys think that's hilarious and begin flapping their arms. Obviously they've never had a calorie concern in their skinny lives.

"According to Grace, the modeling agency said that for her height, she could weigh no more than ninety-five pounds," I inform them, "and that's what she weighs now."

"Yeah, right. Maybe without her bones," Keith comments.

"Mrs. Fuhrman stands a better chance of modeling than Grace," Matthew says. "She's got more the looks for it. I'll bet she could steer a car with her chest."

Keith picks up his cup of Jell-O. "Here's to diet food." He leans back and sucks it up with a loud snort.

"Eeeuw, gross," Abby complains.

While everyone is talking, I notice a boy sitting by himself three tables away. He's sipping his soup and taking slow, small bites from a grilled cheese sandwich. "Who's that?" I ask.

Abby glances quickly over her shoulder. "Probably some-one new."

I watch him for a moment. It must be awful, I think, to be all alone like that. Everyone else has someone to talk to. He must feel left out.

I'm thinking about getting up and going over to talk to him, when Abby reads my mind. "He's probably fine, Kat. Really."

Matthew looks at the boy. "Uhh, Kat. That's not—"

"No, it's—" Tim starts to say.

I don't let them finish. I walk toward where the boy is sitting. On the way I'm muttering, "Pretty uncaring and insensitive."

"Hi," I say, as he looks up from his soup. I sit down and am about to add, "Welcome to our school," when I suddenly realize that he looks familiar.

"Hi, Kat."

"Larry?"

He nods. "Have a nice summer?"

"You look different, Larry. What—"

"Growth spurt, different glasses, and"—he rubs his hand across the top of his bristly head—"this is my summer hair-cut." He takes a small bite of the greasy toasted cheese sandwich, then wipes his fingers on his napkin. "Guess you haven't noticed me three rows behind you in science."

"No, sorry, I haven't." I wonder, and I'm sure Larry Greenblat wonders, what I'm going to say next. Out of the corner of my eye, I see Matthew, Keith, Tim, and Abby grinning at me.

"Larry, hi," a voice says behind me. I turn and see Ronald Whitman standing with a pile of books in his arms and his lunch bag perched on top. "I stayed after class to talk to Mr. Torpsky about those ratios he showed us." Ronald sits down next to me, looking confused to see me there.

"With sine, cosine, and tangent," Larry says.

Ronald opens a carton of juice. "Using the Pythagorean theorem."

They both turn to me.

I smile weakly. "What? You expect me to comment on that?" I'm stuck. Snagged. Wedged between two whiz-brains with mechanical pencils and calculators poking out of their pockets, discussing things only the few select geniuses in Mr. Twerpsky's super-duper extra-advanced class understand.

". . . the equivalent proportions—"

". . . simultaneous homogeneous equations—"

". . . in simplest radical form—"

My brain's been on vacation. Why hasn't theirs? To prove I'm not a total twit-head, I reach for Ronald's dessert, a square of apple crisp. "Look," I say, holding it up. "Pie are squared!"

Larry and Ronald both give startled blinks and then nod politely.

"Well." I stand and grin broadly. "I just stopped by to say hi. Nice to see you two."

"Bye," they both say. As I walk away, I can hear, "You have to find the sine of the complement of angle B."

Everybody is laughing when I get back to my table. "I guess that wasn't a lonely new boy, huh?" Abby says.

"Or a troglodyte," Matthew adds.

"No, but *thank* God"—I smack the table for emphasis—"I went over there. Those poor guys were *so-o-o* stuck on their math. They don't know Pythagoras from Pinocchio. Pitiful." Despite the looks I'm getting, I go on. "Those are two baffled and bewildered boys. But I balanced a couple of lopsided equations for them."

I hear Keith whisper to Tim, "She's pretty good in math, but those guys are certifiable geniuses. She knows that, right?"

I ignore Keith and stand, making believe I'm holding an award plaque. "I'd like to thank the Academy of Mathematicians . . ."

"*Cut!*" Abby interrupts. "Nice try, Kat. But face it. You're impetuous. You leap before you look. You're impulsive." She puts her arm on my shoulder. "But there are worse things you could be."

I'm not so sure. Larry and Ronald may be too polite to say anything, but Mrs. Whiezersky sure isn't going to hold back.

8

AFTER SCHOOL, I STOP AT THE MAILBOX
and bring the pile of envelopes and catalogs into the
kitchen. Mixed in with the bills are two envelopes that
might be invitations or something. Both are addressed to *The
Randall Family*. One is from the Animal Rescue League and
the other is from someone named Lawrence. I leave them on
top of the pile.

Hannah is at school late again. The house is quiet. Empty.
I pace around for a while, checking for snacks, picking up
magazines, not able to concentrate. Finally I decide to deal
with my bicycle debt. I count my money again, hoping that
it has magically multiplied. Since it hasn't, I decide to go
across the street to speak with Mrs. Stafford.

When I tell her I'm looking for baby-sitting jobs, and any
other work she might have, her face lights up and she
decides on the spot to go to a Saturday-night movie. Score
one plus-point for my money-earning project. Score one
minus-point for my social life.

Mom and Hannah are home when I get back. Mom's got

news. "We received a letter from the Lawrences," she says, holding up an envelope.

"Who are the Lawrences?" I ask.

"Mrs. Lawrence is the person who was driving the car that hit Cheddar," she explains. "Her husband has asked if they can visit."

"Visit *us*? Why?" I ask. "Mom, the woman practically killed Cheddar."

"Isn't it a bit much to ask?" Hannah says.

"It may be a little out of the ordinary, but I believe their concern is genuine."

"Maybe they're afraid we'll sue," Hannah says.

Mom gives her a look.

"Well, that could be it," I say. "Anyway, do they really have to come here?"

"I believe that allowing them to do so is the right thing," Mom answers.

"Then when is this visit happening?" I ask. I don't want to be home.

"At about eleven tomorrow morning," Mom answers. "Both of you, please do your best to be gracious."

When Mom uses that tone, we know she's serious about manners. And I know where I have to be tomorrow.

❧

Dad is working outside when Mr. and Mrs. Lawrence arrive in the morning. When he opens the front door and shows them inside, I recognize them right away. They'd been at the veterinary hospital, and I'd spoken to them by the front door.

Mr. Lawrence recognizes me. "This young lady was just arriving at the veterinary clinic as we were leaving recently, and we spoke. That's correct, isn't it?" he asks me. I nod.

They are dressed nicely. Mr. Lawrence is wearing khaki pants, a blue shirt, and a blazer. Mrs. Lawrence has on a navy blue skirt with a floral blouse.

At first it seems like a regular social visit. Everyone is polite. But on the inside, polite isn't exactly what I am feeling.

Mr. Lawrence then brings up the subject of the accident. He begins by saying how sorry he and his wife are. He asks how Cheddar is doing and says that they would like to take care of any veterinary bills that result from Cheddar's injuries.

Mrs. Lawrence looks sympathetic. Then she startles us by saying, "How did the accident happen?"

No one knows what to say, how to answer the question. Mr. Lawrence puts his hand on his wife's. Looking at her, he says, "We know how the accident happened, Ann. We spoke about it on the way over."

Mrs. Lawrence looks embarrassed as she reaches into her skirt pocket and pulls out a note. She reads it, and then says, "Oh, yes. I do know. And I am very, very sorry."

Mom answers, "We understand that it wasn't intentional."

"Oh, no, I'm sure it was not," Mrs. Lawrence says.

Hannah glances at me.

Dad stands up and says, "May I offer you some iced tea?"

"Thank you," Mr. Lawrence answers. "That sounds very nice."

While the others are talking, Mrs. Lawrence picks up her brown leather purse and looks through it. She pulls out a number of tissues and several slips of paper, which look like more notes. She puts them all away, and then a few minutes later, she opens the purse and looks at the papers again. She sips her iced tea, smiles, and adds comments about the fall flowers and the weather we're having.

Mr. Lawrence clears his throat. "We don't want to take up too much of your Saturday morning. We just wanted to let you know how sorry we both are about the accident. Ann was apparently uncertain where she was and was reaching for something, perhaps in her pocketbook, when she hit your dog."

Mrs. Lawrence looks down and then at her husband. "The roads all look so similar in this area. Don't you think?"

"Yes, they do," Mom agrees. "It's easy to mistake one for another." She smiles at Mrs. Lawrence.

Mr. Lawrence stands up and asks if he might speak with Mom and Dad in another room. Mrs. Lawrence seems unsure about what she's expected to do. She begins to follow them to the dining room, but Mr. Lawrence takes her arm and brings her back to where Hannah and I are sitting. "Ann, it would be nice if you would visit with these young ladies for just a few more minutes. I will be right back."

Mrs. Lawrence sits down again. For an awkward moment, no one speaks. I break the silence. "Where do you live, Mrs. Lawrence?"

She hesitates, twisting the handle of her purse, and then answers, "Over on the road by—you must know it. Near the river. I'm sure you have been there. It's a popular road."

Hannah and I nod as if we know just where she means. I can't help feeling sorry I asked her something she has trouble with.

Mrs. Lawrence asks where we go to school and what we are studying. Hannah tells about high school and about all the extra activities she has signed up for. I know I should contribute to the conversation, so I tell about troglodytes. While I'm talking, Mrs. Lawrence opens her purse, takes out her wallet, and looks at her identification card. When I finish talking, she looks up and says, "Frogtown Road. That's it. Number sixteen. That's actually where *he* lives. My family lives in Lowell. My parents have a house on Oak Street, on the corner."

I can tell by Hannah's face that she is doing the same quick math that I am. Checking to see if Mrs. Lawrence's parents could still be alive. Neither of us says anything.

Mr. Lawrence, Mom, and Dad return from their talk, and the Lawrences say good-bye. Mrs. Lawrence pats me on the shoulder and tells me to have a happy day.

Mom and Dad sit down to talk with us after the Lawrences leave. "As you must have figured out, kids, Mrs. Lawrence is very, very confused," Dad says. "We were told by

Mr. Lawrence that she has been seen by doctors recently because of her deteriorating memory."

Mom shakes her head. "It's a very sad condition."

"Why was she driving? She shouldn't be driving," I say.

Dad explains that Mrs. Lawrence had not driven in some time, but that she found a set of keys and took the car while Mr. Lawrence was outside in the backyard. The experience was not only dangerous, but it was frightening for both of them.

"Frightening because she got lost?" Hannah asks.

"Yes," Dad answers. "She was very scared and confused, and David Lawrence was frantic when he went into the house and realized she had taken the car. He said he knows now that she cannot be left alone, not even for a short while."

"It's lucky Cheddar wasn't killed," I say. "How long has Mrs. Lawrence been like this?"

"It's come on gradually," Mom answers. "This sort of thing happens to some old people. It goes by different labels—Alzheimer's disease, senile dementia. But it's likely to progress over several years until finally it becomes obvious to all that it has reached a severe stage. It's terribly sad."

I think of my grandparents and begin to worry. "But it doesn't happen to *all* old people, right?"

"No, not all."

"She really wasn't sure why they came today, was she?" Hannah says.

"I don't believe she was," Mom agrees.

"I'm pretty sure she's even mixed up about where she lives," I add. "She said something about living with her parents in Lowell."

The phone rings, and it's for me. The Staffords have decided to go to an early movie and are leaving in an hour. Mom asks me to take the laundry out of the dryer and fold it before I go. I head downstairs to the laundry room.

While I'm folding, my mind is going double time. Part of me wants to scream that Cheddar was practically killed and it never, ever should have happened. I'm not the only one to blame. Mr. Lawrence should have hidden the car keys. He's got to watch her as if she's a little kid. He can't turn his back on her. Another part of me wonders what it feels like to be Mrs. Lawrence and to be so confused.

Mrs. Lawrence and I have something in common . . . we've both gotten ourselves in trouble for taking a vehicle we shouldn't have taken. And we're both lucky that the outcome isn't even worse than it is. We've got something else in common, too—memory issues. She can't remember, and I can't forget.

9

"WHY DO YOU SMELL PERFUMY?"
Mom asks, as I come downstairs, ready to baby-sit. "Aren't you just going over to the Staffords?" She looks at me and adds, "You aren't expecting any visitors while you're there, are you? That's not a good idea."

I sigh impatiently. "Mom, I know that. I'm trying to keep myself from absorbing the smell of Winston and his snacks. He's always gnawing on salami or pepperoni or some type of stinky thing. It makes everything around him smell like a sour burp."

Mom leans back against the counter and smiles. "It can't be that bad."

"Get close to him sometime and take a sniff," I say, pushing open the door. "But I need the money. Be back in a few hours." I stop and turn. "I *do* still need the money, don't I? No one's called about finding the bike?"

"Sorry, no," Mom answers. "You need that job."

"Too bad. See you later."

When she opens the door for me, Elspeth is wearing turquoise blue eye shadow, dark red lipstick (not quite inside her lip lines), and blush. As soon as her parents leave, Elspeth whispers to me that she's been reading a magazine meant for teenagers.

"Really? How'd you get it?" I ask.

"From my cousin. She's older." I can see Elspeth is trying to sound grown-up. It's hard for me to keep a straight face looking at the overdone makeup.

"How old are you now, Elspeth?"

"Nine. I'm in fourth grade now," she says proudly. "Winston's in third. *I* have Spanish now and *I* get *lots* of homework." She points to a pile of schoolbooks.

Trying to act cool, Winston saunters into the family room, wearing baggy, oversized shorts and a hockey jersey. "Yo." He turns on the computer. The Staffords must be out of sausage. Winston has a chunk of cheese that smells like feet.

"Kat, I'm sorry Cheddar got hurt," Elspeth says.

I nod. "Me, too. She's had a hard time, but she's getting better. I'm hoping she'll be home in a few more days. What was Cheddar doing over here that day, anyway? I heard a commotion."

"Snacks," Winston says.

Elspeth explains. "We brought our snacks outside to eat on the steps."

I get an instant image of Cheddar's nostrils quivering, of her digging madly, and of her chubby body squeezing slowly underneath the fence and finally popping free.

"Yeah, then your crazy dog came charging after us," Winston adds.

"We ran around the car, but she just kept chasing us, so we got in the car and honked," Elspeth says.

"What were you eating?" I ask.

Elspeth shrugs. "Just cheese and pepperoni."

"That would do it," I say.

Elspeth smiles. "She's a funny dog. I like her."

Winston leans toward me and sniffs. "You smell pretty good." Then to his sister he says, "Hey, El, Mom bleached our fish."

I stare at him, thinking about what he just said. "What?"

"She bleached our fish," he repeats casually, his eyes on the computer screen.

Elspeth jumps up and hurries into the kitchen. I'm behind her. There on the table is a goldfish bowl, with two belly-up white fish floating in it. "Uh-oh," Elspeth whispers.

"What happened?" I ask.

Elspeth looks sad as she explains that the bowl and pebbles on the bottom had gotten scummy. Her mother decided to take out the fish for a few minutes while she cleaned everything with bleach.

I stare at the almost transparent fish. "I guess she must not have rinsed all the bleach out. They didn't used to be white, did they?"

She shakes her head, looking solemn. "They're *gold*fish. One was mine. Her name was Gertrude. The other was Winston's. That was Schmoo. Winston stopped paying attention to him." Elspeth's lips begin to quiver and she grows silent.

"Well, maybe we ought to do something with them, Elspeth. We could bury them," I suggest, putting my arm around her shoulder.

"My friend flushed his," Winston calls from the other room.

"That doesn't seem very nice or respectful. I'll help you bury them, Elspeth." I take her hand. "Come on, let's find a place to dig a hole."

Elspeth is quiet as we get a trowel from the garage and find a spot to bury the fish on the edge of the property, near the forsythia bushes. While she's digging, I look at her unhappy little made-up face. The turquoise eye shadow is smeared.

We walk inside and drain the fish bowl into the sink, pouring the limp, ghostly fish into a paper cup. Back outside, as the fish slide down the side of the cup into the ground, I hear Elspeth whisper, "Good-bye, Gertrude. Good-bye, Schmoo."

After we cover the hole with dirt, Elspeth lays a couple of black-eyed Susans on top. "There," she says with a sigh. "Is that all there is to do? Should we sing something?"

I think for a minute, not sure what to suggest. Then Elspeth says, "How about 'Day Is Done' or maybe 'Linger.' They're songs from Junior Girl Scouts."

I think about the fish. 'Done' seems appropriate. The idea of them lingering, ghostlike, bothers me. So together we quietly sing "Day Is Done."

"I think they had a nice burial, Elspeth. Let's sit on the swings. You can tell me about school."

We sit side by side and talk. "It's boring. We keep doing last year's math over and over. And my teacher blows her nose all the time," Elspeth says, starting to pump higher.

I smile at Elspeth. "Probably allergies. It shouldn't go on all year. And neither should the math review."

The swings are low. I drag my feet on the ground and sway from side to side. Little does Elspeth know that reviewing math and having a teacher with a running nose are not, as problems go, biggies.

"I can't wait to get to seventh grade," Elspeth says. "Don't you love it?"

I shake my head. "Not yet, I don't. This year has *not* started off well. But it should get better soon." I look at the dirt on the knees of her jeans. At her age, I always had dirty, bruised knees. And a life that was pretty uncomplicated.

I stand up. "We ought to go inside and see what Winston is doing." Elspeth jumps from her swing, landing on her feet.

When we walk into the family room, Winston looks up with his cheeks full. Elspeth spots chocolate crumbs on the table in front of him. "Hey, you aren't supposed to eat Mom's brownies!"

"Hummmm?" he answers, swallowing. "Who said?"

"Mom did, and o-o-o-o-oh, you're going to get punished." She sits firmly on the sofa. "Those brownies are for Mom's meeting."

I think for a moment. The way my luck is going, I'm going to get in trouble for not supervising Winston enough and allowing him to eat off-limits food. "Is there any more brownie mix around?" I ask.

Elspeth hops up on the counter and opens the cabinets. "Nope."

"Then I'd better call my house and see if we have any." Dad answers and says we're in luck. I tell Winston to sit on the front steps and not move a millimeter while I run across to my house and get the mix. Then the kids and I start making the brownies.

We discuss whether to mention the new brownies to their mother, or just add them to what's left of the old ones and hope that they pass for hers. Winston wants no mention of the new brownies. Elspeth wants to tell. I have the tie-breaking vote. I decide to be truthful. Winston then figures he may as well eat more brownies, since he's going to get into trouble anyway.

We follow the recipe on the back of the box, and, except for having to stop twice to talk about cooperation, and then again to pick some eggshells out of the batter, we get the mix into the oven pretty quickly. The smell of the brownies baking is an improvement over the smell of Winston's cheese.

Winston complains about having to do the dishes, but with me standing right by, prodding him and checking on quality control, he finally gets them done.

The Staffords walk in while we're stacking the new brownies on top of the old ones. "Hmmm . . . smells good in here," Mr. Stafford says, sniffing the air. Mrs. Stafford looks confused when she sees the brownie platter, piled higher than when she'd left it.

"Winston ate a lot of your brownies without asking," Elspeth announces. Then she smirks.

"How was I supposed to know they were for a meeting? You didn't put a *Keep Off* sign on them. And how come you never make stuff like that for *us?*" he asks. I know what he's trying to do and I watch to see what his mother will say.

She sighs and waits a moment, probably counting to ten, before answering.

Deciding to explain, I say, "I'm sorry that I didn't know he was eating them until it was too late, but I'm pretty sure that the brownies we just made are good."

"They look fine, Kat. Don't worry about it. And thank you for so quickly replacing what Winston ate. You should take the extras home with you."

With Winston scowling at that suggestion, I say, "No, keep them, please. The kids did a good job helping to make them."

~©~

Walking across the Staffords' front lawn toward my house, I look at the money I earned. I've got a long way to go before I can pay for a new bicycle. It's going to take time. Time that's going to include things like brownies and fish funerals.

10

I WAKE SUNDAY MORNING WITH the Whiezersky bike deadline glaring at me. I call Abby and Matthew to see if they want to go with me to look for the bike. Matthew says he has already checked a few places, but he'll come along anyway. We arrange to meet at the end of Richmond Hill Road.

Matt's waiting as I huff and puff to the top of the hill, then get off my bike to catch my breath. Abby comes coasting along from the other direction a minute later.

We discuss where to look for the bike. "How about over by the movie theater?" I suggest.

"Been there," Matthew answers.

"Then how about the park?" Abby asks.

"Been there, too," he says. "And I've been to the library and the train station."

"Ahhh, but have you been to Pie in the Sky Bakery?" she asks.

Matthew raises his eyebrows. "No. Why?"

"They've got the best cookies," she says, matter-of-factly. "I vote we begin there."

"Come on, Abby. This is serious," I say. "I think we should go back to the veterinary hospital to see if the person who took the bike brought it back."

"Kat, the chances of anyone, other than you, returning a stolen bike are slim. Besides, I'm sure the people who work there are keeping an eye out for it," Matthew reminds me. "Let's ride over by Main Street and look there." We stop three times to look at bicycles outside stores. Even if the bikes are the wrong color, we figure we should check them. None look like Melody Whiezersky's. We look behind the hardware store, then down the alley between Bakin' Bagels and the bank. We ride around the elementary school and then behind the municipal building. A row of police cars is next to a garage.

"Hey," Matthew says, pointing to the garage. "I'm pretty sure that there's stuff stored in there that the police find around town and no one has claimed. My dad took me to an auction there once and they had bikes."

"Then shouldn't we go into the police station and ask if we can look in there, just in case?" Abby suggests. "Maybe Melody's bike is there and no one noticed it's on the missing bike list."

"You never know, something like that could happen. Let's ask," I say. So with Abby pointing out that it's pretty ironic that none of us brought a lock, we leave our bikes leaning against the wall by the entrance to the police station.

Behind a high counter, a policeman sits at a desk talking on the phone. The name badge pin on his shirt reads

Sergeant Tiani. I grow nervous waiting for him to finish—a reaction, I think, to the police badge, uniform, and revolver. When Sergeant Tiani ends his phone conversation and looks up at us, I'm quivery.

"Kids, can I help you?" He takes off his glasses and leans back in his creaky chair.

"Yes," I answer in a voice that doesn't sound quite like mine. "I'm looking for a lost bike. And by any chance, are there bikes out in that garage?" I turn and point in the direction of the garage. "And can my friends and I possibly check for the one I'm trying to find?"

"When did you lose your bike?" he asks, picking up his pen.

"Last Wednesday. I parked it outside the veterinary hospital. The bike wasn't actually mine. It was borrowed. But then it disappeared. And we three have been looking for it, but haven't found it, and we thought that maybe it turned up and got put in there." I point to the garage again. "Can we look?"

His chair creaks again as he tips back. "The bicycles in the garage are ones we have no records on. So you're saying that this bike you're looking for was not reported stolen. That right?"

Matthew speaks. "No offense, Sir, but we thought maybe it could have been put in there without someone knowing it had been reported. Mistakes can happen."

"That is correct, they can," Sergeant Tiani says. "So, you're saying that there *is* a record of this bike's disappearance. And you're just double-checking, in case we haven't been doing our job here."

I swallow hard. None of us says anything. I wish this man would be nicer. Maybe smile once.

"I'll need your names," Sergeant Tiani says, "to check the file."

"The bike belongs to Melody Whiezersky," I say. "Whiezersky is the name you need."

He looks at me. "That's a start." He walks to a row of filing cabinets. Flipping through the folders in the last drawer, he pulls out a file. "All right. Here it is." He opens the folder, puts on his glasses, and begins to read. "Sounds like the bike you described. Disappeared from the animal hospital. Now I'll need your names." He looks at Matthew first. "Name?"

"Matthew Mease."

"Excuse me, but these two are just helping me find the bike," I start to explain. "Abby and Matthew are—"

"And you're—?" Sergeant Tiani interrupts.

"Kat Randall."

"Ah, yes. I see you're linked to this case," he says, tapping the report. "You want to elaborate on what happened?"

I clear my throat. With my voice shaking, I begin my story. When I get to the part about taking the bike from the bike rack at school, the officer interrupts me. "So, you stole the bike."

Sweating, I answer, "Not really. I *borrowed* it. Then someone stole it from me before I could return it." The words aren't even all out before I know how ridiculous they sound.

Sergeant Tiani takes notes and says, "Uh–huh" a few times. "Uh-huh, skipped school. Uh-huh, took the bike."

Then he removes his glasses, looks at me, and says, "Any other trouble with the police? I can check that," he continues. "A few other bicycles are missing around town. Know anything about them?"

What kind of person does he think I am? "No, I don't. And I wouldn't. I didn't even steal this one. I explained that. I would have brought it back."

"Technically you stole it, Miss Randall," he says.

"But Officer, Sir," says Abby, "I've known Kat practically my whole life. She's honest and—"

"And you're—?" he asks Abby.

I cringe. I hate that Abby and Matthew are being pulled into my mess.

"Abby Quinn."

"Sir, it's important that you really understand that Matthew and Abby have nothing to do with this bike, or any other missing bike," I say.

"Uh-huh. And Miss Randall," he replies, "it's important that *you* really understand that you now have a police record."

Stunned, I swallow hard.

Finally, Sergeant Tiani goes with us to the garage to look for the bike. A few other bikes are there, some whole ones and some with parts missing. But no Whiezersky bike. And if that isn't bad enough, before we leave, we have to practically sign in blood that our own bikes are really our own.

We ride home a lot quieter than we'd set off earlier. "Well, at least now I know for absolute sure that I have to earn a bundle of money. Time's up. No bike. And I know that the police have me on their list of suspicious characters." I try to hold back tears.

"Sorry, Kat," Abby says sympathetically. "I'll help you earn the money, and I'm sure we can make Sergeant Smileyface believe you're not a thief."

"Yeah, when they figure out who really took the bike, he'll feel like an idiot for giving you such a hard time," Matthew says.

"Look, you two don't have to worry about this. It was all my stupid mistake," I say. "I'm the one who has to deal with it."

Mom and Dad are reading the Sunday *Times* when I get home. I sit down on the couch next to Mom and take a deep breath. Then I tell them what happened. When I'm done, Dad sighs the sigh he makes when he's not happy. "First, it's ludicrous for anyone to suggest that you might know about other missing bikes. That has to be cleared up." He takes off his glasses and rubs his eyes. "Second, we'll have to pay for a new bicycle. The agreed upon deadline is here. The Whiezerskys want a bike."

Mom nods. "You'll have to speak to the Whiezerskys and find out what they paid for the bicycle and where they bought it. They should have the choice of getting another bike themselves or asking us to get one and deliver it to them."

"All right," I say, feeling awful. "I can't believe that this whole mess just keeps getting worse and worse."

Mom shakes her head and speaks in her exasperated-but-trying-to-sound-calm voice. "Kat, we're extremely troubled by all this. Especially now that a police officer has said you might be implicated in other bike thefts. This is not child's play. And you're learning how complicated one serious error can get."

You can say that again. With dread, I walk slowly toward the phone to make the call. Mrs. Whiezersky answers. My worst nightmare. "I'm not surprised that your little escapade turned out like this," she says, with a sharp edge to her voice.

I explain that we can either mail a check tomorrow or buy a new bike and deliver it. Whichever she wants.

Mrs. Whiezersky sighs and acts as if even replacing the bike is unacceptable. Finally, she tells me what the bike cost and where I should send the check. "You were incredibly thoughtless to have created this situation. I hope your parents are making you live with some stiff consequences." I cringe at the thought of the ones she could come up with.

❧

If Cheddar were here, she'd listen to my problems and make me feel that I'm not a total wretch and disappointment. I lie on my bed and think about her, about her aches and pains and her poor leg. My head is a mangled mess of thoughts—carelessness, blame, mistakes. "Come home soon, Cheddar," I whisper. "I could sure use some advice. And I'll be so careful. I won't let you get hurt again."

11

I WATCH FOR ABBY, STANDING with my arm inside my homeroom and my body in the hall. Mr. Griff has a rule that some part of the student has to be inside the room in order to be marked present and on time. Keith is leaning out into the hall next to me with his right foot in the room.

"Oh, my gosh," Grace mumbles, squeezing past us through the door. "Have to get those notes out of my locker. Just found out there's an English quiz today." She tears down the hall and is back in a flash, still muttering to herself. "Gotta cram." I turn and watch her tumble into her chair and open her English book. Cram, cram, cram. She flips through pages of her book.

Over his shoulder, Keith calls, "Hey, Grace, that's not all. There's a quiz in math today, too." I see him look over at some other boys. Then he rubs his hands together gleefully.

"*What!* You've got to be kidding. How come I didn't hear him say that?" Grace wails. She jumps up from her seat and rushes to where Mr. Griff is reading the newspaper at his desk. "Mr. Griff, I have to run to my locker one more time. Let me go, please? I'll be fast, promise." Keith and I step out of the way as she bolts out of the room. "My mom's going to kill me," she wails.

In less than a minute, just as the bell rings, Grace is back. Staring at her open math book, she looks like she's about to cry. She keeps checking the clock and chewing her nails.

I look down the hall one last time, then walk over to Grace. "Grace, are you sure—"

"S-h-h-h," she replies, holding up her hand like a traffic cop. "Don't speak."

"Grace, I don't think—" I try to say, but I'm interrupted by the laughter of Keith and the other boys.

Grace looks up and glares. "Will you guys *shush?*"

They keep it up. Keith is practically falling off his chair howling. His hair flops as he rocks back and forth laughing.

"Hey, Grace. If you don't know the stuff by now, you're dead meat," another boy calls out. Then he gives a snorty laugh. Every boy in the room thinks it's funny.

Grace finally catches on. "You guys are jerks!" She pounds her desk with her fist. "You know that? Total jerks."

"Hey, they're just being morons. Don't take it too seriously." I can see that she's coming unglued.

"Easy for you to say, Kat. I mean, you know that stuff without studying anyway," Grace replies. "I don't get math *at all*. I'm going to fail. They think it's funny. Well, my mother's not going to think it's funny. There's no way I'm going to make it through the year." She flips through the pages of the math book. "Look at what's in here. The stuff's impossible."

"It doesn't look so bad," I say.

"It does, too. And I can't believe that we're not allowed to get help from our parents," she snaps. "That's *so* unfair. I'm not going to be able to do it by myself. There's no way." She has tears in her eyes as she starts chewing her nails again.

"Maybe an easier math class would be better," I suggest.

She shakes her head. "No, my mom wants me in high-level groups. She insisted." Grace stops and swallows hard. Then she looks right at me, pauses, and asks, "Will you help me?"

It's my turn to swallow hard. Grace is the most annoying person I know. I don't think I could stand working with her.

"Grace . . ." Out it comes. Out of my blurtful mouth. "If it gets really bad—really, really bad, you can ask me." I can't believe I just said that.

Within seconds, Grace has scheduled a time for me to help her. And within minutes, Abby hears about it.

"What do you *mean* you're helping Grace Fuhrman with math?" Abby sputters. "That's the Grace Fuhrman who drives us nuts, the Grace Fuhrman who tattles to teachers, and the Grace Fuhrman who flirts with Tim! My Tim." She waves her index finger wildly. "Where's your loyalty, Kat? What are you *doing?*"

Good question. Wish I knew.

∽୭∾

Abby is still mad at me at lunch. "Are you crazy? Tutoring Grace! The other day when you talked about earning money, Kat, I didn't think you'd go after it so desperately."

I stand there, holding my lunch bag. "Abby, the tutoring thing isn't about money. Not that I don't need it. But she was a mess. Crying even."

Abby sits down hard, scowling. "Look over there. Grace seems to have recovered." She points to where Tim stands at the cashier's counter. "See? See that?" Grace is switching places with another girl and is now right behind Tim.

I lean forward and say quietly, "But he hasn't even turned around. He's not paying any attention."

"Maybe not now, but it could happen, you know. She could wear him down, and then he could start spending time with her," Abby answers, under her breath.

Matthew arrives, unaware that he's in a tense zone. Tim finishes paying for his lunch and sits down with us, hitting his knee on the table, as usual. "*Ouch.* Hey, did you hear what happened to Ronald Whitman in gym this morning?" Tim asks. "He wore a cheap blue shirt and then sweated when we had to run the mile. The dye ran and turned the top half of his body bright blue. What a dweebis."

Abby and I aren't in the mood to laugh, but Matthew and Tim think it's pretty funny. Matthew talks about the time he borrowed Ronald's class notes to study from. "That kid's mind is so amazing that I needed Cliff Notes to understand *his* notes. Talk about brains."

"Maybe *he* could help Grace," Abby says, talking into her turkey sandwich, "with her math."

Tim looks up, stopping in mid-chew. His left cheek bulges with hoagie. "Why would he want to do that?"

"She's lost already. Doesn't understand a thing," I explain. "And since Mr. Billings doesn't allow parents to help, maybe—"

"But *Grace?* She's obnoxious," Matthew says. "She'd drive you nuts."

Abby gives me a look. I'm not sure if it's a what-did-I-tell-you look or a thank-God-Tim-didn't-offer-to-help look.

Walking next to me as we leave the lunchroom, Matthew says, "How'd your parents take the news about our visit to the police station?"

I'm about to tell him, when I catch a glimpse of Melody Whiezersky going into the girls' room. "Matt, I'll talk to you later. Gotta catch that girl. That's Melody. It was her bike."

Melody and I are not the only ones in the bathroom. Two sixth-grade girls are combing their hair in front of the mirror. "Hi, Melody," I say. The two girls watch curiously, glancing back and forth between Melody and me. They must have heard about the bike.

Melody looks up as she dries her hands. "Hi." She looks small inside her loose-fitting overalls.

Neither of us says anything else until the girls finally walk out. "Melody. I'm very sorry about everything. I was hoping that we'd get your bike back by the weekend."

"I was, too," she says quietly.

"It might still turn up. Then you could have two bikes." I smile. "If that happens, you can sell the new one and keep the money."

"Look, I'm okay about it. You said you meant to bring the bike back and I believe you. My mother's really mad, though. She gets . . . she can be . . ." Melody stops. Maybe she doesn't want to say anything bad about her mother.

"I just hope you don't think I normally do things like take bikes."

Melody is about to say something when the loudspeaker blares, *"Katia Randall to the office. Katia Randall to the office."*

12

MRS. LANDES POINTS TOWARD
Mrs. Eliaz's office door. Like a robot, I walk through it and
stand in front of Mrs. Eliaz's desk. Her dark blue suit looks
like a military uniform and fits her large frame neatly. If she
bought the suit to look principal-like, she has achieved that
effect. "Sit down, please, Katia," she says. "There is something we must talk about."

I don't know whether I should keep quiet or blurt out expla-
nations for every stupid thing I've done since school began. I
can feel my jaw opening, shutting, opening, shutting, as I try to
figure out whether to speak or not to speak. I must look like a
goldfish. If Mrs. Eliaz didn't know that something was the matter with me before, she sure knows it now.

"Katia, a problem has arisen." Fingering a gold pen, she
turns it slowly as she speaks. "Do you know what I'm referring to?" She raises one eyebrow and it disappears beneath
her dark bangs.

Opening, shutting, opening, shutting. If I answer "No," it
would be because I'm not sure which of my problems she

knows about. If I answer "Yes," I might accidentally end up divulging a problem she doesn't know about. Saying nothing seems best, even if it's kind of rude. I sigh and hope she goes on talking before I have to.

She does. "Well, it seems that there is a growing problem with bicycles at school."

I cringe, then nod, knowing that I'm snagged on this one. "I really messed up last week. I can explain what happened." My voice quavers. As I tell her the story, and watch that pen turning in her hand, I think of a pig on a spit, turning over a fire at a barbecue. I look up at her every so often. She just nods for me to go on.

"So the bike was first borrowed, by me, then stolen, by someone else," I say, finally summing things up. "My parents have sent the Whiezerskys money for a new bike and now I'm working to reimburse my parents. And I told Melody I was really sorry. That's about it."

"Not quite," Mrs. Eliaz says, shifting in her seat. "Another bike has disappeared from the bike rack." She stares at me hard. Maybe she's looking for telltale signs of guilt.

I just stare back. My mind is racing. Who told her about me in the first place? The police? Mrs. Whiezersky? Doesn't it matter that I don't need someone else's bike now? Is this what happens to people with police records?

"I don't know anything about any other bike," I say. "I really don't." My eyes are stinging.

Mrs. Eliaz lifts a paper from her desk. "Well, I was compelled to speak with you. There was a complaint from Mrs.

Whiezersky." She taps the paper in her hand. "We would have had this talk sooner, but I have been out of the building for a couple of days. Now that another bike is missing, it's important that we clear things up as best we can." She leans forward in her chair. "Katia, is there anything more you can tell me?" The eyebrow goes up again.

"About a second missing bike?" I ask, hoping that she isn't also referring to my leaving school early. "No. Nothing." I look straight at her, but she looks blurry through the tears welling up in my eyes.

"Okay, then," she says, dropping the pen on her desk and getting up. "We're done for today. You may return to class. Please ask Mrs. Landes for a late pass."

I wobble away from the office. With the back of my hand, I wipe my wet cheeks. Mechanically, I get my books from my locker and head for French class. I feel as if I've been stung by some enormous bug.

All heads turn toward me when I open the classroom door. Anyone who heard my name over the loudspeaker would be curious about why I was called to the office. I hand Madame Liotard my late pass and sit down.

"What's up?" Matthew mouths quietly.

With so many people staring at me, and with Madame Liotard waiting to continue, I just open my French book.

"*Vingt, s'il vous plait, Mademoiselle* Randall," says Madame Liotard.

"*Merci*," I answer quietly, not looking up.

I barely hear the lesson. All I know is that it has something to do with *l'automne* and other things connected with seasons and weather. If Madame Liotard wants to embarrass me, she could call on me; it has to be obvious that I'm not all here. Just before class ends, Madame asks something about *froid*. While waiting for an answer, she looks in my direction. I just look back. She lets it go. Then the bell rings.

"*Adieu!*" she chirps.

Relieved, I get up and move toward the door. But Madame Liotard follows. "*Il y a quelque chose qui ne va pas?*"

I'm not up to figuring out what she means. I wait for her to translate. "Something is wrong, Katia? May I help?"

I shake my head. "Thank you. But I'll be okay. I just have some things, some problems . . ." My voice trails off as I walk away.

Matthew is waiting outside the door. "So what happened in the office?"

"Mrs. Eliaz wanted to ask me about a missing bicycle."

"You mean Melody Whiezersky's?"

"No, not only that bike. Another one is missing. I'm a suspect, because now I have a record. I can't believe how bad things have gotten, Matt. In such a short time, I've gone from being a kid who just had to get to the animal hospital in a hurry to being a suspected bike thief."

"That stinks. But it can be cleared up. You've got friends," he says.

"Well, one very important friend's furious with me right now. I doubt she'll want to help."

"What are you talking about?"

"This morning I accidentally agreed to help Grace Fuhrman with math, and that really ticked off Abby. You've seen Grace flirt with Tim, right? It really bugs Abby."

"Oh, come *on*. Tim like Grace? Get serious," Matthew says. "Abby's wasting energy on that worry. See you later."

Matthew walks home with me after school. "This day has been a nightmare," I say as we cut across the lawn in front of my house and turn up the walk. "Being a juvenile delinquent is stressful. It feels like my name is covered with slime. Like toxic waste is coating it."

"Nice image, Kat," Matthew says. "Sounds like a case for 'Slime Busters.' But don't worry, I've already talked to Tim and Keith and a bunch of other kids about what really happened."

The phone is ringing as I open the front door. I hurry to pick up. It's Mr. Lawrence, asking how Cheddar is doing. I tell him she is improving and that we're hoping she'll be home by early next week. I'm about to hang up, when I hear Mrs. Lawrence get on the line. She startles me by inviting me to come to tea on Saturday morning. She says to bring a friend. I'm not sure if she means Hannah. Hannah isn't going to be home on Saturday, and I say so. Mrs. Lawrence tells me to come anyway and to bring another friend. Before I know it, I accept.

"Why the surprised look?" Matthew asks. "Who was that?"

"Mr. and Mrs. Lawrence. First Mr. Lawrence—he wanted to find out how Cheddar is doing. And then Mrs. Lawrence got on. I'm pretty sure Mr. Lawrence didn't know ahead of time what she was going to do. She asked if I would come to their house for tea on Saturday, with a friend. It was confusing. But I said yes. So Matt . . ." I give him my most pleading look.

He shakes his head firmly. "Forget it. Uh-uh. I don't do tea."

"But Abby's so ticked off at me, she'll never go."

"Yeah, she will. Give her time. If you're really going to do it, she'll come along."

Matthew is quiet for a moment, then he says, "So, *are* you really going? I mean, how weird is that, to be going for tea with someone who drove her car into your dog but doesn't know it. It's crazy. Like the Mad Hatter's tea party."

I think about Mr. and Mrs. Lawrence. "I'm going to go, Matt."

❧

Dad gets home. He's just gotten praised for a news story he wrote and is in a great mood. He says hi to Matthew and then asks me about my day. Here goes his good mood.

I would give anything to be able to report what a model, gold-star daughter I am. But instead, I have to tell him about my session with Mrs. Eliaz. "Dad, it was humiliating—being suspected of taking another bike. Is this going to keep happening every time something's missing?"

He sighs. "Unfortunately, you're learning fast what happens when a person's integrity is questioned."

"You mean my honesty? Dad, I *am* honest. I really am. I'm not a thief, and I don't think it's fair that one stupid mistake has led to this. My reputation's in the sewer."

"Then, Kat, it's up to you to pull it out of there, isn't it?"

13

GRACE CALLS AFTER DINNER AND I
spend an hour and a half on the phone trying to help her
understand her math. She starts off sweet and appreciative.
That turns to frustrated and whiny, and finally ends in bit-
terness, toward the "stupid" math book, our "unfair" teacher,
her "demanding" mother, and "smart" me. I'm about to say,
"Look, Grace. You better get someone else to help," when
she starts to cry.

"This is (*sniff*) impossible for me (*cough*). I'm not (*sniff*)
smart in math." She blows her nose loudly.

"You'll get it," I say, trying to insert my phrases between
her sniffs. "Sometimes things take a little time."

"Mr. Billings might not (*sniff*) give me all that much
time." She clears her throat and then adds, "You'll help
again, right?"

I cringe and hesitate. "No" would get me out of the
situation. But Grace is acting as if she's ready for a break-
down. "No" might send her over the edge. Then I'll have
to add that to my list of thoughtless moves with serious

repercussions. "Yes" would make her feel better, but keep Abby angry longer.

"Well?" She blows her nose again. "Will you?"

"But Grace, what about help from Mr. Billings? He's trained to explain."

"But I don't want him to know that I don't get it. I might get dropped to a lower math group. My mother will kill me."

"Okay, Grace, okay," I say, not wanting to deal with the issue of her mother.

When she finally hangs up, I collapse on my bed and let out a dramatic moan. "Trouble, trouble, trouble." Without thinking, I reach my arm under the bed to where Cheddar always lies. I'd give anything to be able to put my face against her fur and soak up some affection. Despite my blunders, she loves me. Why can't people be more like dogs?

Staring up at my ceiling, I notice one of the cracks in the plaster is in the shape of an A. It's a sign—the sign of the crack. I should call Abby. Taking a deep breath, I dial. "Abby, I know you're mad." I shoot the words out as soon as the phone is picked up. "And I understand why. But here's what happened." I race ahead quickly, before she has a chance to think about hanging up.

I'm starting to explain Grace's shaky self-confidence, when Mrs. Quinn's voice cuts in. "Whoa, Kat, wait a minute! I can't get a word in. Wow, you can talk fast! Do you even breathe?"

"Oh, I'm sorry, Mrs. Quinn. I thought you were Abby."

"Hold on. I'll call her."

Waiting, I have a chance to get really nervous. Abby might have time to decide she won't talk to me. When she gets on, Abby doesn't sound very enthusiastic, but I plow ahead. I begin again, telling her how I got roped into helping Grace, describing Grace's iffy mental state, the pressure from her mother, her feelings about being stupid, the crying. "So, you see? I got stuck."

Abby doesn't speak for a moment. Finally, she sort of grunts. Then she mutters about what a pain it is that Grace, of all people, is playing on my sympathy. But she admits that she can see how I got trapped.

Relieved, I tell her about the rest of my day, especially the principal's office part. And I tell her about tea with the Lawrences.

"What? You're not serious?" she asks.

"Uh-huh. Look, I know you're only just barely not mad at me. Timing isn't good here, but please, Abby, will you come with me to the Lawrences?"

She waits a moment. "Oh, all right. Someone's got to see that nothing else goes wrong."

Good point.

14

ABBY AND I STAND ON THE
Lawrences' front porch on Saturday afternoon and wait for
someone to answer the doorbell. We both feel awkward and
nervous. And we're both wearing nice clothes.

Standing there, the tension is getting to me. We're too
serious. I try for some tea-related humor. "Did I ever tell you
what I used to think when my parents were listening to
Handel's *Messiah* and the tenor was singing 'Comfort Ye'?"

Abby shakes her head and rolls her eyes. "What?"

"I thought he was inviting people to 'Come for tea.' And
I couldn't figure out why he sounded so intense about it."

We're both grinning when Mr. Lawrence opens the door.
"How are you, Kat? Welcome." I introduce Abby. Mr.
Lawrence smiles warmly and shows us into the living room
where Mrs. Lawrence is sitting, holding a plate of assorted
cookies on her lap. "Ann, you remember Kat. We visited
with her not too long ago at her home. And this is her
friend, Abby."

Mrs. Lawrence smiles and holds out her hand. "Nice to meet you."

"And how is Cheddar?" Mr. Lawrence asks. "Is she improving?"

"Yes, thank you. We can't wait for her to come home." I glance around the room at the antique furniture and the framed photographs. "Are these your children?" I ask Mrs. Lawrence.

She puts the plate of cookies down. Leaning close to the pictures, she says, "Well, let's see. I imagine it's . . . ." She picks up a photo of what looks like younger versions of herself and her husband, standing in a yard with two children. "Off to church in Lowell. It's quite a family, isn't it? My father is a deacon in the church on the hill."

Mr. Lawrence puts his hand on Mrs. Lawrence's shoulder. "Actually, Ann, although that may look a bit like the yard in Lowell where you grew up, this photograph was taken right here on the side of this house. It was an Easter Sunday many years ago." He reaches for another picture of the same two children and holds it for me to see. "Our daughter and son are now grown. Both live several hours away and have busy careers."

Abby and I look at each other. I can't imagine what it would be like to be confused about my own family. I think of my grandparents and pray it never happens to them.

Mrs. Lawrence nods and turns to me. "Well, now, how close by do you live?"

"Pretty close," I answer, not reminding her that she'd visited us at our house. "About a mile."

"I was thinking," Mr. Lawrence suggests, "that we might like to take advantage of our remaining mild weather and move outside to the terrace in the back."

Mr. Lawrence leads the way out through a sliding glass door. Mrs. Lawrence carries the plate of cookies. We step onto a flagstone terrace, where there are wrought-iron chairs and a table and lots of potted red geraniums.

"This is beautiful," Abby says, when she sees the river only about twenty-five yards from the house. "It's so pretty being right by the water. Do you fish?"

"When I can," Mr. Lawrence answers, glancing at his wife, then quickly looking away. "But I don't get to it as much as I used to."

"When it's my dad's turn to pick our family vacation, it always involves fishing," Abby says. "Fishing can be fun."

Mrs. Lawrence holds out the plate of cookies. "Would anyone like a sweet treat?" She smiles cheerfully. "I believe that we also have drinks. David, we have, haven't we?"

"Yes, we do," he answers. "The choices are: hot tea, iced tea, cider, and ginger ale. What is your pleasure?"

Cider is everyone's choice. "I'll help you," I offer.

"Wonderful," Mrs. Lawrence says. "We'll go inside together." She gets up and walks to the back door, stopping to pinch off some dead blossoms on a geranium along the way. When we reach the kitchen, Mrs. Lawrence hesitates for a minute, then says, "Ah, yes." She walks to the stove and turns on a burner under a teakettle. Then she opens a cupboard and reaches for cups and saucers. "Let's see, how many are we?"

"Four," I answer, thinking how to shift our beverage from tea to cider. "It's a warm afternoon. How about cider?"

"Do you think so? Yes, I believe that's a good idea. And it's quick, as well." As she opens the refrigerator, I turn off the burner.

"Where would I find the glasses? I'll pour for you," I offer. We set up a tray and carry the drinks outside. Abby and Mr. Lawrence are talking about the river.

We look toward the water as we sip our drinks. "I never tire of the river," Mr. Lawrence says. "It's soothing, yet powerful, and all the while magical."

"I know what you mean," Abby agrees. "My dad says the water washes his stress away, and that fishing is cheaper than therapy."

Mr. Lawrence laughs. "He's right. You know, girls, I have a thought that may appeal to you. On Sunday afternoon, Ann has been invited to go shopping with an old friend from college. During that time, when I will be a temporary bachelor, I could take you out in our canoe. It's right in the shed over there and seats three. And we could fish if you like."

Abby's eyes light up. "That would be fun, don't you think, Kat?"

"Sure," I say, a little surprised that Abby is into fishing. She's never said much about that.

While we're making plans to do that, I hear a whistling sound. At first I think it might be a river bird or other small creature. I see Abby cock her head and know that she hears it, too. "Excuse me," I say, "but what's that whistling?"

Mr. Lawrence stops and listens. Then he looks at Mrs. Lawrence. "Do you hear that, Ann? It sounds like our teakettle whistle."

Mrs. Lawrence glances quickly at our drinks. "We're having cider, David. I shouldn't think the teakettle would be on." She smiles at us.

I stand up, realizing that Mrs. Lawrence must have turned on the stove burner again. "I'll go check. Be right back."

Returning, I say, "You know, we were so busy talking in the kitchen that, without thinking, we must have just flicked on the burner. Kind of an automatic reflex."

Mr. Lawrence smiles at me. "Thank you, Kat."

❧

Riding home in Dad's car, Abby and I are both pretty quiet and thoughtful. "Well? How was the visit?" Dad asks.

"Interesting," we both answer at once.

"And sad," I add. "Mrs. Lawrence is so mixed up, and she really needs to be watched. Abby, did you see her give a smile when Mr. Lawrence asked about the teakettle? It's almost as if she's the patient one and he's the confused one."

"You two are nice to spend time with the Lawrences," Dad says. "Under the circumstances, your visit could be considered very out of the ordinary."

"Guess so," I answer. "But we're going back."

"Really? How's that?" In the rearview mirror, I see Dad's look of surprise.

"Mr. Lawrence has a canoe and he invited us to go out on the river with him tomorrow afternoon. We're going to fish."

"Well, for heaven's sake," Dad exclaims. "Our journeys certainly have unexpected twists and turns."

You can say that again.

15

WORK, WORK, WORK. MONEY, money, money. Between raking our front and backyard, and then baby-sitting for the Staffords, I feel like a worker bee. But at least it feels good to be shrinking my debt, which I've decided to call the "Big D." Abby left me a homemade card in our mailbox, with a picture of her holding her nose, cleaning out the Foleys' cat's litter box. Inside the card were sixteen dollars and the message "No backsies."

Sunday morning I work on bagging leaves, twigs, and grass clippings. It's a grubby job. One of Cheddar's old soggy tennis balls is in with the debris. I brush it off and save it for when she comes home. I've also been making sure that we're stocked up on her favorite foods. I'm planning her homecoming meal. Soup to cheese.

When it's time to go fishing with Mr. Lawrence and Abby, I'm more than ready. Except that, compared to Abby,

I look like such a fishing rookie. I've got all this stuff on my head—hair clip, sun visor, sunglasses. She has a sporty green hat with some sort of fishing apparatus dangling from it. She says it's her lucky lure. And she's even got her own pole and tackle box. I'm impressed.

The aluminum canoe isn't heavy. We carry it to the river, then bring down the paddles, fishing poles, tackle boxes, life jackets, and a thermos of juice.

"Careful climbing in." Mr. Lawrence reaches out to me. "It's tipsy."

The canoe and I both wobble as I step down. "Sit in the center of the seat and try not to move about too much," he says.

"Life jackets, everyone." Mr. Lawrence hands us each one. The orange color clashes with my red sweatshirt.

We go with the current, so paddling is easy. Mr. Lawrence sits in the back of the canoe and paddles. He watches for a good spot to fish, and I think about how relaxed he looks in his floppy, worn brown hat and rumpled fishing vest. We glide through the water until Mr. Lawrence says, "Let's try over there," pointing to a place at a river bend, just past some rocks and riffles where the water looks deep. Tree limbs hang out over the water. It's the kind of place Hannah and I used to pretend was a hideaway for gnomes.

I lower the anchor and watch it disappear into the dark river. A fish jumps not far from us. I make a fish face and a kind of kissing sound.

"What are you doing?" Abby asks.

"Calling the fish," I answer. "Duck hunters call ducks. Turkey hunters call turkeys. Can't fisherpersons call fish?"

Abby rolls her eyes. "Oh, brother."

Mr. Lawrence laughs, and I'm happy to see him having fun. He hands me a pole and offers me a choice of gummy trick-or-treats for fish. I pick a wiggly thing that smells like pumpkin. Abby attaches her lucky lure to her line and casts out into the water as if she really knows what she's doing.

I, a fish out of water, am at a loss as to how to catch the fish *in* the water. Mr. Lawrence patiently shows me how to cast and reel. I want him to enjoy his own time on the river, so I do my best fisherperson imitation.

There's no one else around. It's peaceful watching the leaves and branches floating by. I rescue a wet monarch butterfly that's clinging to a maple leaf, then watch its strength slowly return as it dries out on top of our juice thermos. We talk quietly about random things and identify the water birds. I can understand why Mr. Lawrence describes the river as soothing.

For a few moments, I close my eyes. The rocking motion of the boat on the water reminds me of times spent swaying in my favorite branches of our sycamore tree on a breezy day.

I'm almost asleep, sitting there with the pole in my hand, and am startled when Mr. Lawrence clears his throat and says, "I don't know how much you two might know about Alzheimer's disease. It's what's causing my wife, Ann, to be so confused. The symptoms have been coming on gradually. At first, people outside the family were unaware, but now, as you know, it is clearly noticeable. She can no longer be left alone."

"Is there anything that can help? Medicine?" I ask.

Mr. Lawrence reels in his line and casts his lure back into the water as he answers. "There's a lot of research. Some of it is encouraging for the future, but not for the people whose brains are already damaged by the disease. We have tried one drug that has been approved for use, but it helped for only a short time."

"Aren't there other drugs to try?" Abby asks.

"None that are likely to help her. Sadly, Ann's condition will probably continue to worsen," he says.

"I'm so sorry, Mr. Lawrence," I say. "It must be really hard."

"For both of you," Abby adds.

"Well, it's all right," he answers, forcing a smile. "Ann is good-natured and loving. We've been together for fifty-four years. She has done a great deal for me during that time, and caring for her is what I do now."

"I'll be glad to come over sometimes," I offer. "I could spend time with Mrs. Lawrence so you have a chance to do something you want to do."

"Your offer is kind, especially after all you've been through with your injured dog. But as I said, caring for Ann is what I do now, and that's fine. I brought up the subject of the disease only to help explain." Mr. Lawrence takes off his hat and smooths his gray hair. "Hey, I saw one jump out there." Pointing to the middle of the river where the current is swift, he suggests, "Let's pull up the anchor and move out a bit." Mr. Lawrence is ready to change the subject.

What must it be like for him, day after day, trying to help clear things up for his wife? I stare at the monarch, now beginning to move its wings, as I think about Mrs. Lawrence, and about the pain Mr. Lawrence must feel as she drifts away.

Not wanting Mr. Lawrence to think he made me sad, I take my pole and, with a flourish, whip it back over my right shoulder and then flick it forward. My wild whipping goes awry. To the shock of us all, there, suddenly dangling off the end of my pole, is Mr. Lawrence's floppy fishing hat. I gasp. "I am *so* sorry!"

Mr. Lawrence chuckles as he reaches up and unhooks his hat. "No harm done, Kat. I've caught a few unexpected things in my day. Got my brother Lou's ear once."

I feel better. But once we actually begin to catch fish, I realize I haven't thought through the whole fishing thing. I'm not happy about the way the little lips look with hooks sticking in them. When I catch my first fish, a rock bass, I apologize as I let him go.

"You think it's a he?" Abby asks.

"Sure. *Shes* are too smart to get caught," I answer, firmly.

"You may be onto something," Abby agrees.

We catch what I'm told are four perch and one small-mouth bass after that, and I'm relieved when they're released into the river.

Paddling back is difficult since we're going against the current. Abby and I take turns helping Mr. Lawrence, and we make it before the sun sinks too low and it grows dark. I step onto the bank with the monarch clinging to my finger; then I find it a new resting place on a protected branch of a dogwood tree.

⤳֍⤸

Mom picks us up, and we're just pulling out of the Lawrences' driveway, when Mrs. Lawrence and her friend return from their shopping trip. We wave to Mrs. Lawrence, but she doesn't seem to recognize us.

She gets out of the car and walks toward the house, carrying a small shopping bag. Mr. Lawrence greets her by the kitchen door.

As our car pulls away, I look back, holding them in my view as long as I can.

16

I COLLAPSE INTO MY SEAT IN
social studies, out of breath from rushing to my locker for my notebook. Grace taps me on the shoulder. "I've been trying to get to talk to you."

I know that. It was just a matter of time before I'd be snagged. What's it going to be like when we get to really hard math?

"The third, fifth, ninth, and last homework problems are impossible. I don't get that stuff about variables in both sides. And now we've got more for homework again. I tried to call you on the phone last night."

I know that, too. Hannah shielded me, and gladly, because it meant more of her own personal phone time.

"So, were you sick?" Grace goes on.

"No. I couldn't come to the phone."

"Grounded from the phone?" she probes.

I shake my head. "Nope. Just had stuff to do with my parents." That's pretty much true, because I did spend time with them discussing the "Big D," now at about ninety-five dollars, and thinking of more jobs I could do. When I suggested they hire me to put a new roof on the house, we all knew my desperation was getting ridiculous.

"So when can you help me?" Grace asks.

I figured that was coming.

"So when are you stealing your next bike?" someone else says.

I turn quickly. Dennis Boyle smirks. "Did you sell the parts off the last one?"

Stunned, I feel as if someone has punched all the breath out of me. My face is turning either red or white, I can't tell which. My answer is stuck somewhere between my brain and my throat. I just stare at him.

It's Grace who speaks. "You're a jerk, you know that, Dennis? What makes you think you can say a stupid thing like that?"

By now other kids are listening. It feels as if the whole room is leaning toward me. I turn to Dennis and say slowly and firmly, "I did *not* steal a bike."

"That's not what I heard," Dennis replies. "Someone told my mother that you took her kid's bike, right from the school bike rack. That right?" He jingles the chain hanging from his belt.

"Get serious, Dennis," Grace says. "You're wrong."

I look Dennis in the eye and answer him. "When I say I didn't steal a bike, I mean I didn't steal a bike."

He challenges me. "So this lady's kid's bike *wasn't* stolen? She's lying?"

Mr. Creston stands by the door talking to another teacher. I lower my voice. "The bike was stolen, yes. But—"

"Mind your own business, Boyle," Matthew cuts in. "You don't know the facts."

"Facts? There actually *are* facts?" Grace asks, clearly not about to mind *her* own business, either. "What are they?"

Mr. Creston clears his throat. "Please cease the chatter, and the unpleasant-sounding tones coming from over there." He waves his hand toward my area. We get quiet and he begins class.

About ten minutes into the period, when Mr. Creston is writing on the board, Grace taps me on the shoulder and hands me a note:

What was that about with Dennis???
I know you didn't steal a bike,
but what happened?
Tell me, pleeease!

I turn and mouth "Later."

❧

For the rest of the school day, I keep my head way into a book and try to look too busy to be interrupted by anyone who might bring up the subject of bike theft. It's awful thinking that every conversation I see might be about me. Abby and Matthew do their best to cheer me up. Without them, the seesaw balance of good/bad for this year would look as if an elephant has plopped its big bottom down on the bad end.

~∾~

"You want to help me at my house?" Grace asks at dismissal time. "The Library Media Center isn't open after school today, and I sure don't want to use Mr. Billings's room, or any room near his."

"I keep telling you, Grace, Mr. Billings is the best person to ask for help. Just because you have questions doesn't mean he's going to instantly drop you to a lower math group."

"I can't take that chance," Grace says, starting toward the front door of the school. "So's my house okay? It's only three blocks from here."

"Fine. But I have to get home before four-thirty. That's when we're getting my dog from the vet." We walk through the crowd of kids waiting for the second bus run and across the side lawn. I wonder how many kids are talking about me. I'm sure I hear my name.

"So, you've *got* to tell me what Dennis was talking about," Grace urges. "I know he's full of it, but what *was* all that?"

I don't feel like confiding in Grace. But I'm stuck. If I dodge the issue, it'll seem as if I'm hiding something. And besides, she defended me outright, without knowing anything about the situation.

I sigh my pre-story sigh and begin. "Something I did turned out horribly."

Grace's eyes widen at what she hears, and except for the times when she gasps, "Oh, my gawd," or "How horrible," or "No way," her mouth merely gapes open in amazement.

"Dennis makes it obvious that the whole thing isn't going to just quietly go away. Lots of people have already heard about it. That kind of news spreads like poison ivy. They've got to be wondering about it, and me."

When I was seven, I rigged up a daredevil device in the backyard. Sort of a flying trapeze–type thing. A few kids who tried it got scraped up, slamming into the trunk of the sycamore, and their parents wouldn't let them play with me for a while. I wonder if kids are going to be warned to stay away from me again.

"Kat, most people aren't idiot-jerks like Dennis. Everybody else likes you. It's too bad a scuzzball like Dennis has the bike information, but you've got friends who'll explain what really happened." She pauses and adds. "I know I will."

❧

Grace's house is tidy. It's cream colored with slate blue shutters, and along the front are shrubs that look as though they've been cut with a barber's electric trimmer. Two identical pots of white plants sit on either side of the front steps. In all the places where my family would have lots of random flowers growing, there's a covering of reddish brown gravel.

"I'm home," Grace calls from the front hall. We carry our backpacks into the dining room and leave them by the table.

I phone Dad to let him know where I am and check about going to get Cheddar. He decides to pick me up at Grace's and we'll go from here.

We walk into the kitchen, where we find Grace's mother standing in front of the refrigerator. "Kat and I are going to do homework together," Grace says.

Mrs. Fuhrman smiles that smile parents get when kids say they're going to do schoolwork. Then she asks, "Would you two like a snack?" Quickly, she gives us our choices before we can answer. "We have carrot sticks, apple slices, cucumber spears, and rice cakes." She stands with her arms folded in front of her like some sort of no-nonsense crowd-control official in designer clothes. Her hair is lightened beyond blonde.

"Mom, isn't there anything else? Cookies, chips, or something?" Grace looks embarrassed.

"No, that's it. For drinks, we have diet soda, unsweetened iced tea, sparkling water, and lemonade."

We go with the apple slices, rice cakes, and lemonade. When her mother goes upstairs, Grace says, "Sorry about the crummy snacks."

"No problem. My mom is very into healthy eating, too, so I'm used to not having junk food." That's true. Mom and I are both vegetarians and we eat a lot of grains, beans, fruits, nuts, juices, and seeds. Dad and Hannah pretty much eat the same thing, give or take a few bacon cheeseburgers.

"I have a feeling it's different," Grace says under her breath, as we open our math books and take out paper.

I let her remark pass. "Okay, let's start with the problems you had trouble with last night, the equations with variables on both sides, even though we went over them in class. You want to be sure you understand."

Mrs. Fuhrman comes into the room with a handful of newly sharpened pencils. "Here, use these. You can't do math with dull, stubby pencils." She leans over the table, "Let's see, how far have you gotten? Need help?"

"Mom, please," Grace says. "You aren't *allowed* to help."

"Kat, I suggest you change to that chair on the other side of the table. The light's better," Mrs. Fuhrman points out.

"Mommmmmm," Grace pleads impatiently. "Leave us alone."

Mrs. Fuhrman shrugs. "Sorry. Just trying to help." She smiles at me and backs out the door.

Grace rolls her eyes. "She can't leave me alone. And she's always checking up on me."

"What for?" I ask.

"Everything. Calories." She looks uncomfortable. "Mom makes sure I don't eat a lot. Because of modeling."

"Where are you modeling?"

"Nowhere yet, but my mother keeps trying to set me up with an agency in New York. A friend of hers has a daughter modeling there and Mom's been calling and sending them pictures. She's obsessed about it."

"What does the girl who's modeling say about it? That it's cool and glamorous and all that stuff?"

"I have no idea. I've seen her picture in a few store ads, but I've never talked to her. Mom thinks it's great, though, and at first I thought it might be cool. But now I figure that if the agency was interested in me, they'd say so. And the way Mom's bugging me about food, I'd just like to forget it."

"When would you go into New York, if the agency did want you to model?"

"Probably during the school day or in the afternoon. Either way, I'll miss something. I mean, I'm not brainy enough to be able to miss class work and still get good grades. And Mom wants to make sure that I'm a cheerleader, too, because she was one. She doesn't get that I can't do everything. I just can't."

Feeling bad for her, I say, "No one can, Grace."

She looks at me. "Some people, you being one of them, probably can. Things are easier for certain people. Not me."

"It only looks easy from the outside, Grace. Think about the day I had today with Dennis announcing that I'm a thief. Throw in the money I owe for the bike. And worst of all, my dog's hurt. I've got as much junk to deal with as anyone."

Grace looks astonished. "I always thought you had it all, Kat. I figured everything was a snap."

"Hardly," I answer. "Trust me, I've got stuff."

17

I'M EXCITED AND NERVOUS—
excited that Cheddar will soon be home, and nervous about
doing the right things to make her comfortable and not let
her get hurt again. Before the accident, she trusted me. I
hope she will again.

Dad and I smile when we see Cheddar standing. She
almost manages a smile back. I put my arms around her
and congratulate her for doing such a good job of getting
better.

"Can she walk on the cast?" I ask Dr. Goldstein.

"She won't put much weight on it for a while," he
explains. "She'll hop on three legs at first, then gradually
she'll start to use the injured leg again."

"Do you recommend that we put a plastic bag over the
cast when she goes outside?" Dad asks.

"When it's wet out, sure. We'll be checking the cast every
week and will probably change it in a couple of weeks, so it
actually won't get too nasty."

We get some more instructions and make an appointment for Cheddar to come back to see Dr. Goldstein. Then it's time to go. Right off, I want to carry Cheddar, but Dr. Goldstein advises that we give her a chance to try walking first. I hate seeing her having a hard time. When we finally reach the door, Dr. Goldstein says, "Okay, good. Now you can give her some help and carry her to the car. And whenever she has to cope with stairs, give her a lift."

I ride in the backseat with Cheddar, telling Dad to watch out for bumps in the road, and praising Cheddar for her bravery. Mom and Hannah have just gotten home, and they rush to greet Cheddar. Even Winston and Elspeth run across the street to see her. Winston has cheese.

Hannah and I help Cheddar inside and use my old Raggedy Ann comforter to make a soft nest for her in the kitchen. Her water bowl and some snacks are right next to her, and she can be part of our activities without having to move much. She'll sleep downstairs in the kitchen until she's stronger and more steady. It'll be a while. I can't wait to have her back upstairs in my room—where she belongs.

We eat dinner in the kitchen instead of the dining room, and when we're through, Mom and Dad stay at the kitchen table, reading the newspaper. I sit on the floor doing my homework next to Cheddar. Hannah reads a magazine on the other side. No shortage of family togetherness for this dog.

Later, when the phone rings, Hannah answers and calls for me to pick up. Expecting it to be Abby, Matthew, or even Grace, I say, "Hel-l-l-o-o-o-o" in an exaggerated way. I'm surprised and embarrassed when the person who speaks isn't any of them. It's Mr. Lawrence.

"Oh, I'm sorry, Mr. Lawrence," I apologize. "I wasn't expecting . . . I mean, I was kidding around."

He laughs. "Humor is good for the soul." He clears his throat. "Now, the purpose of my call is to discuss a subject that came up briefly while we were fishing."

Did I say something I shouldn't have? Nervously I wait for him to continue.

"You mentioned the possibility of coming to the house with the idea of spending time with Ann. I've since thought about that, and in light of the fact that my Retired Men's Club meeting is tomorrow afternoon, I wonder if you might be available. I would, of course, insist upon paying you."

"Oh, no, Mr. Lawrence," I say, pausing for a moment over the money issue. "I mean, yes, I'll be glad to do it, but no money is necessary."

"It absolutely is," he replies emphatically. "Although Ann need not know about it." I understand that he doesn't want her to feel as if she needs a baby-sitter.

"What time do you want me there?"

"My meeting begins at four-thirty. How would arriving at four suit you?"

"That's fine. I need to stop home after school to see my dog first. Then I'll ride over on my bike."

"Well, that's good then. You'll be doing me a favor by letting me pay you. If it works out for you and Ann, I could then ask you again, without feeling that I'm imposing. It would be nice if you could help Ann collect seeds and snip some plants to root inside for the winter. Gardening is something she still feels comfortable and confident doing."

I hope I won't do something to hurt their plants.

"Just one more thing. Tell me about Cheddar's progress. Is she coming along well?"

We talk about Cheddar for a while. I can tell that he is still feeling bad about her. We say good-bye and I sit down by Cheddar. Stroking her head, I say, "Cheddar, you don't mind that I'm spending time with someone who hurt you by accident, do you?" *Thump, thump.* "I'm not doing it for the money. They need someone. I've botched up this year, but maybe helping the Lawrences is something I can do right."

18

SCHOOL IS TORTURE. KIDS IN MY homeroom suddenly get quiet when I walk in. But not before I hear Marsha say, "So, you think she did it?" My cheeks prickle and I can hardly breathe in that room. In gym, Ms. Cohen has an odd expression when she calls my name to climb the rope. I've never felt more conspicuous in my life than I feel hanging from that rope. All day people are either looking at me or making a point of not looking at me. Every conversation that I overhear seems to be about me.

"You can't tell by looks."

"Who's lying?"

"It belonged to some little sixth grader."

I can't wait to get away from that place where suddenly I'm being looked at as someone else . . . someone who, at the very least, you wonder about.

It feels so good to see Cheddar when I come home. I help her go in the backyard, and then sit by her nest while we both have a snack. With Dad checking on her while he worked at home, she's had company during the day. Already she's losing the smell of the veterinary hospital and is starting to smell like herself. She's napping when I get up to leave. I whisper that I'll be back soon.

The Lawrences are in the front garden when I ride up their driveway on my bike.

"Well, I see you made it here safe and sound," Mr. Lawrence says, smiling warmly and brushing the dirt off his hands.

"Yup, no problem," I answer, turning to Mrs. Lawrence. "Hello, Mrs. Lawrence. It's good to see you again."

She smiles. "Hello."

"Ann, you remember Kat. She and her friend Abby visited us a few days ago and joined us out back for refreshments. We had a nice chat."

"Yes, that was very pleasant," Mrs. Lawrence replies. "How are you, dear?"

I wonder if she actually remembers.

"Kat is going to help you with the gardening this afternoon, Ann. I have a meeting and will be back before it's time to start supper." Mr. Lawrence turns toward the house. "I'll wash my hands and change my shoes. These are my not-very-stylish gardening shoes." He holds up one foot to show me just how old and worn the shoes are.

"David. Don't I have a meeting?" Mrs. Lawrence asks. "Shouldn't I change?" She's wearing a tan corduroy skirt with a blue cotton turtleneck and blue gardening clogs.

"No, my dear," he answers. "We took care of your business earlier and now your plan is to garden. Cold weather will be here soon, and you always like to do a few things in preparation." He opens the door at the side of the house by the kitchen. "I'll be right back."

Mrs. Lawrence begins to wring her hands and is starting to follow him inside. Thinking that maybe I can distract her, I say, "Mrs. Lawrence, will you show me your flowers?"

"Well, yes. I could show you some things." She looks around.

"How about those melon-colored plants by the front porch? What are those?"

"These are fancy begonias," she says, and begins to pinch off some dead blossoms. She talks to me about the plants and says that her father helped her plant them.

Mr. Lawrence comes out with his car keys in his hand. "I'm off. I left the number where I can be reached on the counter. Ann, I'll be back in time to cook our flounder and bake those two fat apples on the counter. You enjoy Kat's company while I'm gone."

Mrs. Lawrence looks nervous again, and I'm afraid she's going to insist on leaving with him. "We have some plants like that at home, Mrs. Lawrence," I say quickly. "Do they come back every year?"

"What?" Mrs. Lawrence looks around and then down at the plants. "No." She leans over. "But you can break off bits and put them in water. They'll grow roots and then you'll have new little plants." Her eyes twinkle and she grins, as if making these new little plants is the most wonderful thing.

"The plant doesn't mind when you pinch off stems?" I ask.

"Oh, no. Trimming does them good. They like it," Mrs. Lawrence answers. "We put the trimmings in water. When roots grow, we'll plant them in a mix of soil and our lovely compost."

"What's in your compost?" I ask, trying to keep her busy so that she doesn't focus on Mr. Lawrence backing out of the driveway.

"Oh . . . let me think. Bits and pieces. Uhhmmm . . . what else? Ahhh yes, what-have-you. Lots of what-have-you." She burrows her hand down into the garden and holds up a handful of dark mix. "Here's a nice sample."

I stare at it for a moment. "I think there's a worm in with the what-have-you. Is that okay?"

She isn't bothered by the worm. "Oh, yes. Worms are good." She places the compost and worm back in the garden.

"Should we put those pieces of plant in water now? And then start work on your garden?" I figure we should stay with the gardening as long as possible.

Mrs. Lawrence pauses and looks around. "Well, then." She stops. "What do you think we should do?"

I remind her about putting the snippings into water. Then, remembering what Mr. Lawrence said, I suggest collecting seeds.

"That would be fine." She walks toward the garden on the side of the house by the kitchen door. "These spider-flowers have seedpods ready to explode."

"All right. What will we put the seeds in? Do you have a container?"

"Well, an envelope works nicely. Let's see, is that right?" She looks embarrassed. "My dear, some things I know so well, but other things I just can't keep straight."

I wonder if she wants to talk about that or not. It has to be so hard, one moment to remember, and the next knowing that you can't. She doesn't say anything more; I let it go. "I'll get envelopes if you tell me where to look."

"Some what? Oh, envelopes. Let's go inside and find some," she says. In the kitchen, she asks, "Are you thirsty, dear?"

"No, I'm fine." I watch to be sure she doesn't turn on the burner under the teakettle. "The envelopes are probably kept in a desk, right?" I ask. "Let's look."

I don't want to seem nosy by opening desk drawers, so I wait while she looks. She rustles through a department store bag on top of the desk. "What do you suppose is in here?" She pulls out a pair of ladies' wool gloves. "I don't recognize these. Never saw them before."

"Maybe you bought them when you went shopping with your college friend last Sunday," I suggest, remembering that I saw her come home with a bag like that.

"I don't believe I've seen any college friends for quite some time, dear. Years. But perhaps someone else left these here." She puts them back into the bag. "Maybe she'll come back for them. Now, what did I want?"

"Envelopes."

"That's right, envelopes. And here we are." She pulls several from the bottom drawer and shakes them merrily in her hand. "As my father says, 'Even a blind pig finds an acorn sometimes!'"

Laughing with her and doing my best to keep things clear, I say, "They'll be perfect for storing the seeds of the spider-flowers by the kitchen door." I write on the envelope what seeds will be in there. I'm shocked when she says, "cleome," the flower's scientific name. That she can remember, but not the day she hit Cheddar?

The pods pop open when we touch them lightly, and the seeds drop into the envelope. "What other seeds can we get?" I pull the pencil out of my pocket to label another envelope.

"Impatiens perhaps," Mrs. Lawrence says. "I think we have those, somewhere." She turns toward me abruptly. "Oh, my, are you thirsty? Should I have gotten drinks? I feel I'm a poor hostess."

"I'm fine. But would you like something? I can get drinks for both of us," I suggest. "Juice? Tea? Cider?"

"Thank you, dear. Whatever looks good to you. We'll enjoy our drinks out here."

At the back door, I turn and say, "I'll meet you on the terrace." I whistle to myself while I get our drinks and think about how it's going well with Mrs. Lawrence. A few minutes later, I walk to the backyard with two glasses of cider.

Mrs. Lawrence is gone.

19

"MRS. LAWRENCE?" I HURRY ONTO the terrace and set the drinks down. "Mrs. Lawrence?" I look toward the garden in the back. Walking quickly around the side of the house, I call, "Mrs. Lawrence, the drinks are ready." There's no sign of her.

I put the drinks down and run to the other side of the house. "Mrs. Lawrence! Mrs. Lawrence!" Then to the garage and potting shed. My heart is racing.

How could she disappear so fast? I hurry to the road and look in both directions. I search the neighbors' backyards. Then I remember the river. The terrifying thought comes to me that maybe she's fallen in. I run along the bank downstream until I know I've gone farther than she could possibly have gotten, and then I run back upstream.

Reaching the shed where the canoe is kept, I fumble with the wide door and throw it open. "Mrs. Lawrence? Are you in there? Mrs. Lawrence?" I slam the shed door and run on, stumbling and tripping over branches, vines, and washed-up debris on the bank.

Remembering that Mr. Lawrence left a number where he could be reached, I turn back toward the house. How am I going to tell him she's gone? Can he even get here fast? 911 is better. I dial. As soon as someone picks up, I blurt:

"My name's Kat Randall . . . Randall . . . R-a-n-d-a-l-l. I'm at 16 Frogtown Road . . . *Frog*town . . . yes, number 16 . . . Gray house, white shutters . . . Mrs. Lawrence is missing . . . L-a-w-r-e-n-c-e. She has Alzheimer's. Alzheimer's. The *disease* . . . Yes, she's missing. I can't find her. Hurry please!" I hang up, feeling my head pounding.

Then I hear a toilet flush. I freeze. Out from the small bathroom off the kitchen walks Mrs. Lawrence. "Well, hello," she says pleasantly, while straightening her skirt.

I stare at her a moment with my mouth open. "Mrs. Lawrence," I finally say, "our drinks are ready out on the terrace. And the police are coming."

She stands for a moment. "The police? For drinks? Well, I don't know about that, but how nice."

I let out a little laugh. Not that things are funny, but I'm so relieved. "When did you come inside to use the bathroom?" I ask.

"Well, I believe I just did that now."

I understand that clearing up the details isn't going to be easy or even possible. She must have come in the kitchen door at the side of the house just when I was going out the back door. "I'm glad you're fine, Mrs. Lawrence."

"And I'm glad you are fine, too." She smiles and turns

toward the cupboards next to the refrigerator. "Now what sorts of snacks do you suppose the police would like?"

"They won't actually be staying for refreshments," I explain. "They just want to check with me about something. It'll only take a minute."

Moments later a police car screeches into the driveway and stops with a jolt. Sergeant Tiani hustles up to the house, not even shutting his car door behind him.

"She's not missing anymore," I say quickly through the screen. "She's right here."

"I thought I recognized your name when the call came in," Sergeant Tiani says. "This must be your month for losing things."

I cringe and hold open the door to let him in. "I'm sorry. I should have called you right back."

"And this is Mrs. Lawrence?" the sergeant asks, looking at her. She smiles politely and holds out her hand.

"Yes," I answer. "We lost track of each other for a short while, and I got scared."

Mrs. Lawrence pats my arm. "There now, no need to worry, dear." She stands close, as if to comfort me.

Another police car pulls up. Sergeant Tiani leans out the door and calls, "It's all right. She's been located. Call in to the station."

"Is this going to be in another report, like before, or . . . I mean, it's just that I'm with Mrs. Lawrence this afternoon, while Mr. Lawrence is at a meeting, and when I turned my back—"

"Oh, dear," Mrs. Lawrence says, patting my arm again, "I don't believe I've done my job well this afternoon."

Sergeant Tiani and I look at each other. I'm afraid he won't know what to think now, but he nods to let me know he understands which one of us is supposed to be watching the other. Maybe he's already heard about Mrs. Lawrence because of Cheddar's accident.

"Got the picture. Glad everything is fine." He turns to leave. "You were right to react quickly, young lady. It was the correct thing to do." He closes the door behind him.

I am surprised that Mrs. Lawrence doesn't seem more startled that the police came. "My, that was a brief visit," she says, as Sergeant Tiani drives off.

We go outside to the terrace, where I left our cider. As we sit making polite conversation, Mrs. Lawrence has no way of knowing how exhausted and relieved I feel.

"Tell me about yourself," Mrs. Lawrence says.

What can I say? In two weeks I've gone from feeling like a person you can count on to one that you probably shouldn't.

"Mrs. Lawrence, just a little while ago I could have told you about myself and it would have made sense. But now—"

She smiles at me, and nods. "Things change, don't they? My father's job used to be such a nice one, but since he's become a judge, we've had some unpleasant times. But we adjust."

Not taking in what she said right away, I go on. "But I want to go back and be the person I was, before everything got so messed up. I—" Suddenly ashamed, I stop. Here I am whining about my problems to a woman who, if she were able to go back, might know her age, her own family, and who this sorry kid is having cider with her on the terrace.

"Going back would be lovely, wouldn't it?" she remarks. "My school days were such fun. One year I skipped a grade, I believe it was sixth. But it didn't matter to my friends and me because several grades were in one classroom. My graduating class was eight pupils. And where are you in school, dear?"

I tell her about my school with more than two hundred kids in each grade. "Maybe your son and daughter went to the same school I'm in."

"Well, I don't know. Where did they go to school, I wonder?" Mrs. Lawrence begins to look uneasy. "Oh, what's the matter with me." She shakes her head. "I just can't—"

"Mrs. Lawrence," I say, changing the subject, "since it's such a pretty afternoon, would you like to take a walk?"

I leave a note for Mr. Lawrence and we head along the quiet road in the direction where there are hardly any houses and I figure almost no traffic. Mrs. Lawrence stops and bends down along the way to pick up colorful maple leaves and horse chestnuts. We watch a formation of geese overhead and talk about the season changing. At a curve, I hear a vehicle coming from behind, so I take Mrs. Lawrence's hand. After the Jeep passes, I wonder what I should do—let go of her hand or wait for her to drop mine.

Neither happens. So we walk the rest of the way like that. We're almost back to the Lawrences' driveway when I feel her soft hand give mine three gentle squeezes.

Maybe things are starting to be all right again.

20

MR. LAWRENCE ARRIVES HOME
about half an hour later, looking happy to have been out
with friends. It would be awkward to speak with him then
about the incident with the police, so I decide to wait and do
it over the phone.

Without Mrs. Lawrence noticing, Mr. Lawrence pays me,
and I start for home. I'm almost to the end of Frogtown
Road, where it crosses a narrow part of the river, when I hear
kids' voices. Curious, I slow down. The kids are under the
bridge, and I can hear them better than I can see them.

"Grab it!" one shouts. "Pull!"

Then I hear a man's voice. "Boys, back up, please. I can
get it." A police car is parked beyond the bridge on the other
side of the river.

I lean my bike against the railing and peer over the side.
Below me, wearing muddy boots, stand two boys, ten or
eleven years old. Next to them, his arm stretching toward
something in the water, is a police officer. He pulls the object
up out of the leaves and muck and onto the bank.

"Awesome!" one boy exclaims.

I freeze, staring down at the mud-caked wreck of a bike. It doesn't look exactly like Melody's bike, but who can tell? Pieces are missing and the paint is smeared with river gunk. Unable to help myself, I call down, "What color is that bike?"

Three startled faces look up at me. The police officer wipes some mud off the back fender. "Maroon," he answers. "This yours?"

I shake my head. "No. I've been looking for someone else's bike. It's blue."

"Better stick around then," the officer says. "Looks like there are more in there."

"Wow," one of the boys says, hopping around, "a bike graveyard. Cool."

The police officer turns to the boys. "Now stay still and don't get in the water. You'll only stir it up and make it hard to see." He climbs up the bank and onto the bridge. *Lieutenant Scott* is printed on his name badge.

"Hi," I say, nervously. "You really think more bikes are down there?"

He nods and walks to his car.

I stand and wait. When Lieutenant Scott walks back from his patrol car, I ask, "How many more bikes are down there?"

"I can't tell," he answers. "It's sure not what I expected. I just stopped a while ago to see what those boys were up to. Thought they'd be after fish, not bikes. Excuse me."

He climbs down to wait with the excited boys. "Help is on the way," he announces.

Before long a second police car pulls up, followed by a truck with a towline in the back. When the door of the patrol car opens, out steps Sergeant Tiani. He walks toward me, shaking his head, probably in disbelief. "Miss Randall, we meet again."

I smile weakly and step out of the way while the truck backs up and positions itself next to the railing. A hook dangles over the water. "Good, Anthony," Lieutenant Scott says to Sergeant Tiani. "Glad to see you brought the grappling hook."

"I heard your call into the station. You said you thought there's a pile of bikes down there. Figured the grappling hook would work best," Sergeant Tiani says. He turns to me. "Bikes. Is that what brings you here?"

"I was riding home from the Lawrences and saw the first bike being pulled up. And I wondered—"

"Yeah. I would, too. We'll know soon enough." He adds, "I don't suppose you know anything about this?"

I feel myself sag. "No, I don't."

Sergeant Tiani nods. "Okay, I didn't really think you did. Just had to ask." Turning toward the driver of the truck, he calls, "All right, Jack. Lower the cable."

Lieutenant Scott and Sergeant Tiani guide the position of the hook as it's lowered. I hold my breath as the big hook catches onto the back fender and hoists a second bike out of the river. The boys cheer from below. When it's close enough for Sergeant Tiani to reach, he unhooks the wrecked bike.

"The color?" I call. "Please, can you check the color?"

He pushes aside a chain that's caught around a pedal and rubs mud from the bar that would have supported a seat, if the seat weren't missing. "This one's black."

The hook goes down again and soon has hold of another bike. I watch for the color. It's red. Then, as the fourth bike rises out of the river and dangles close to us, I whisper, "This might be it." I can see some blue on the front fender. I don't know what to wish for—not have it be Melody's bike, but then maybe never know what happened to it, or to have Melody's bike found. Even if it's a wreck, at least I'd be done with wondering.

When Sergeant Tiani unhooks what's left of the bike and props the frame against the railing next to the others, I bend over and look at it closely. The tires are gone, the gearshift, seat, cables, and chain are missing, and there's no mirror. But as mud-smeared as the handgrips are, I can see that they're red. Then I clean some gunk off the place where the manufacturer's name is printed. *Schwinn.*

But what I see next tells me for sure that the bike is Melody's. On the handlebar are the soggy remains of an *I* ❤ *NY* sticker, held on with red-and-white reflector tape. It's her bike. I'm sure of it.

Sergeant Tiani lifts his hat and scratches his head as he looks at the bike. "Do you think this is the one you're looking for?"

"Yes. Melody Whiezersky's."

"You're having quite a lost-and-found day, aren't you, Miss Randall?"

"I didn't wreck this bike and throw it down there," I say.

He nods. "Well, whoever's responsible must have quite a little business going. Cannibalizing bikes and selling parts."

It's giving me the creeps, wondering who's doing it. My mind races. What now? The Whiezerskys. I'll have to speak with them.

Lieutenant Scott calls up. "Hey, you ready? Let's keep going."

"Yup," Sergeant Tiani answers. "How many more do you think are down there?"

"A couple, at least," Lieutenant Scott says.

"Wow," one of the boys says. "Can we have them?"

"Nope. Boys, stay back," Lieutenant Scott replies.

Eight bikes are pulled up out of the river. "They're as good as ruined, with everything that's missing. It's a shame," Sergeant Tiani says.

"It's a crime," Lieutenant Scott adds. He says that when they get back to the police station, they'll be trying to match the wrecked bikes with the reports of missing bikes so that owners can be notified.

I don't have any reason to wait around anymore, so I ride home. Dad is amazed when I describe what happened. "That's some serious thievery," he says. "I didn't expect anything this extensive."

"Since the police will be calling the Whiezerskys, do you think I have to?" I ask, stroking Cheddar's head.

Dad doesn't answer right away, giving me time to decide. "Well, what do you feel is the right thing to do, Kat?"

I sigh and answer, "I guess I have to call. But I sure hope I get Melody on the phone instead of her mother."

I go upstairs to find Hannah. I feel like talking with her before I face the phone call.

"Jeez, Kat," Hannah exclaims, "first you almost lose that confused old woman? Then you see the trashed Whiezersky bike dragged up out of the river? That's a lot."

She sits down on my bed and looks at me sympathetically. "You're having some year, little sister."

I agree. "Feels like fifty years." I straighten up. "Now I guess I have to call the Whiezerskys. Pray that I get Melody on the line and not her witchy mother."

"I'll cross my fingers and wriggle my nose, for luck," she answers.

"Thanks. And Hannah, nice shirt you have on."

"Thank you." She smiles. "I like it."

"Yup, I liked it, too, when I bought it. It's mine."

"Oh, it is? Oops. Then I'll put it back. Later." She gives a little wave and hurries off.

I make my call. When Melody answers the phone, I raise my eyes to the heavens and whisper, "Oh, thank you, thank you."

"Melody, this is Kat Randall. I want to tell you that the police found your bicycle in the river and that it's damaged. I'm so sorry. Really so sorry."

"The police already called," Melody answers. There's a pause. "My mother told me not to expect good news, so I guess I was ready."

"But probably you were still hoping, the way I was, that it would be all right. The policemen told me that someone must be selling parts off stolen bikes. That's an awful thing to do."

We talk for a while. Then I ask her if she's gotten a new bike yet.

"Yes. Pretty much like my old one. It's fine."

"Thanks for saying that, Melody. I'm really glad it's fine. Well, I just wanted to talk to you myself, to let you know about finding your bike. I'll see you in school."

～❧～

There's still one more phone call to make. "Mr. Lawrence?" My voice is shaking. "This is Kat Randall. Yes, I had a nice time, too. Uh-huh, the gardening was a good idea. Sure, next week again. All right. But I have to tell you something first."

When I tell him about Mrs. Lawrence going in one door when I went out the other, and then thinking I'd lost her, and then calling the police, Mr. Lawrence says, "Kat, you seem like a level-headed, responsible young lady. I know you can be counted upon, now more than ever, to keep a close eye on Ann. Thank you. I'll see you next week."

We say good-bye and I go downstairs to spend some time with Cheddar. I lay my cheek on her furry head. She smells like sleep. "He's right, Cheddar, about my keeping a close eye on Mrs. Lawrence. I can't let anything happen to her. Like a hawk, like an eagle, like an owl, I'll watch her."

21

"YOU GOTTA BE KIDDING," I HEAR Dennis Boyle say. I turn from my locker to see who he's talking to and am surprised that it's Melody Whiezersky. "Of all people, *you* oughta be the most ticked off," he says.

"It's not your problem," she answers calmly. She looks him in the eye. "Besides, it's over." What else can they be talking about but the bike?

Dennis sees me and moves in my direction. "Jeez, Kat— you oughta become a lawyer if you're already this good at beating a rap." He gives a disgusted laugh and raises his arms toward the crowd of kids around us. "Am I right?" He spins, hoists up his baggy jeans, and saunters down the hall.

My face burns. "No, as a matter of fact, you *aren't*," I call after him. "So, butt out!" The crowd stares. I wish I could evaporate.

"What a loudmouth jerk," Melody says, looking embarrassed. "He lives across the street from me. Yelling is what the Boyles do best. His mom talks with mine. That's how he knows about the bike thing. I've known him forever, unfortunately. And I can't stand him or his creepy brother. They make me think of weasels." This is a side of Melody I sure haven't seen before. "That could be because of the ferret Dennis is always carrying around the neighborhood. He's a lot nicer to his pet than he is to people."

"I guess he thinks you ought to hate me," I say. "A lot of people probably think that." I glance around. Most of the kids have walked away. But I'm sure they're talking and telling their friends about what just happened. There probably isn't one kid in this school who doesn't know about me.

Melody pushes her hair back from her face. "Look, I don't hate you, Kat. In the beginning, yeah, I was upset. But now," she shrugs, "it's okay. I've gotten to know you. And you've done everything you could. What more are you supposed to do? Anyway, I'm sick of all the talk about bicycles. You know?"

"I sure do," I answer, as the bell for homeroom rings. "Thanks, Melody. I'll see you."

Melody turns toward her homeroom. Watching her walk away, I tell myself that what really counts is that she, my friends, and my family know the truth.

In math, before I have a chance to talk to Abby about what Dennis said, Mr. Billings announces that we will be tested the next day. Grace draws in her breath with such gasping force that I think she's sucking all the oxygen out of the room. "But that doesn't give us enough time to study!" she wails, once she's able to speak.

Keith turns toward her. "Chill, Grace."

Grace grabs my shoulder. "But we don't *get* all this stuff," she whines. "We'll all *fail*."

"We?" someone in the back says.

Abby leans over and whispers to me, "Guess you spent all that time with her for nothing."

I sigh. Maybe Abby is right. One thing is certain. Grace will be tapping me on the shoulder any second.

Yup. *Tap, tap, tap* (but it's more like *wham, wham, wham*). "Kat, you've gotta save me. Please, oh, please. Can you come over today and help me study?" She's breathing hard, as if she just ran the mile. "Huh? After school?"

I hesitate.

"Kat, *please*," she persists.

I hold up my index finger. "Hang on. Ssh-h-h."

Mr. Billings is explaining what he'll be testing us on. "Variables and equations, properties, reciprocals, transforming equations—"

"Addition, subtraction, multiplication, and division of positive and negative numbers?" Keith asks.

"Sure. Everything up to, but not including, polynomials. In other words, the first three chapters," Mr. Billings says. "So let's take fifteen minutes or so to review."

Grace grips the back of my sweater. "Kat, you'll help me?" A bone in her tense hand cracks next to my ear. "Okay?"

Abby watches to see what I'll say to Grace. I hesitate, feeling pressed, squeezed. Abby wants one thing. Grace wants something else. I haven't had a chance to figure out what I want yet. And there's other homework I have to do besides math. Grace could easily take up most of my time.

Grace is not able to wait another second for my answer. I hear her say, "Tim? Would *you* have time after school to help—"

This time the gasp comes from Abby. And there's a sudden shift of who wants what, and a sudden whipping around of heads to see what will happen next.

"Okay, Grace, okay," I say quickly. "I'll work with you after school."

Limply, I sink in my seat. How weird that one minute Abby thinks I'd be crazy to help Grace, and the next minute Abby'd go crazy if I didn't.

∽∾⊘∾

"Thanks for keeping Grace away from Tim," Abby whispers to me, as we walk down the hall after class. "I'd have been *so* ticked off if she'd gotten him to work with her. She'd flirt the entire time, I know it." Abby puts her arm around my shoulder. "I feel guilty that you're stuck dealing with her again. I owe you."

"It's okay. Grace gets on people's nerves, but when you get to know her, she's not all that bad. She's got a lot to deal with. A *lot*."

Abby looks surprised. "Really? I didn't know. What's going on with her?"

"It's involved. I'll talk to you about it another time. I've got science." I point to Mr. Corento's lab. "See you at lunch."

~~♋~~

Mr. Corento clears his throat to begin what I figure will be another baffling, boring science lesson. He tells us he has a slide show about the theory of evolution. Then he hands out little rectangles of paper with evolutionary illustrations for us to arrange in the right order after the slides. I squint and lean forward to get a better look at Mr. Corento's tie. It looks as if rectangles of paper aren't the only things he chopped. The bottom of his tie is missing.

Being officers in the Audio-Visual Club, Larry Greenblat and Ronald Whitman assist with the slide presentation.

"Let us begin," Mr. Corento says, as the first slide flashes on the screen, "with a look at this simple protoplasmic mass, probably originating in the sea."

The slides continue, showing step-by-step development of new forms. Larry begins to advance the slides faster. Suddenly, among the pictures of creepy, crawly creatures slithering up out of swamps and ponds, flashes an old yearbook picture of Mr. Corento. The class erupts and won't stop howling until he threatens us with detention.

Mr. Corento's nostrils quiver angrily, as if he's detected a foul odor, and he orders Larry and Ronald out into the hall.

foul odor, and he orders Larry and Ronald out into the hall. Now in an instant, they go from being the kind of quiet, almost invisible kids that don't even get a "bless you" when they sneeze, to being seventh-grade heroes. If they have trouble with the change, I can always counsel them about the ups and downs of reputations.

∾ର∽

When I get to the lunchroom, everyone is talking about what happened in Mr. Corento's class. It's all over the school. Now, at least a lot of kids who would have been talking about me are talking about Larry and Ronald. Thank goodness.

"Do you believe those guys?" Matthew exclaims. "Excellent!"

I set my milk down on the table, and Abby makes room for me. "I hear Larry and Ronald have to stay after school and write Mr. Corento an apology," she says.

Tim shrugs. "No big deal. Definitely worth it. Wish I'd been there."

Just then Larry and Ronald walk through the door. They both have a new walk, almost a bop, as they collect high fives all the way across the cafeteria.

"So, Kat, I hear you have a long afternoon of math ahead of you," Matthew says.

I turn to Tim. "Just curious. What would you have said when Grace asked for help? I mean, if I hadn't said I'd do it?"

"You're kidding, right?" Tim answers. He looks toward Matthew and makes a vomit sound. "Anyway, I'm busy after school today. Soccer game."

I sigh. "So, anyone think that I can get Grace to master equations, reciprocals, variables, axioms, properties, and graphing by tomorrow morning?"

"Nope!" comes the resounding answer.

I take that as a challenge.

22

MADAME LIOTARD READS *LE PETIT Prince* in French from a wooden stool in front of the chalkboard. I tune out, picturing Dennis stomping all over my reputation like a professional TV wrestler. It's going to take some doing to change my image. I may have to go overboard in the Miss Congeniality department for a while.

And there's Grace the Super-stressed. I've heard the expression "saving grace," but can this Grace be saved? I look up at the ceiling, as if the answer's up there.

Annie Sullivan taught Helen Keller. Professor Higgins taught *My Fair Lady*'s Eliza Doolittle. But can I teach Grace Fuhrman?

"What do you *mean* 'associative?'" Grace wails. "I don't get it." She thumps her fist on the table. "It means nothing to me. Nothing." Her eyes well up with tears.

I take a deep breath and go over it again. My voice has

taken on a Mr. Rogers tone. "All right, now. Do you see how we can add or multiply these numbers in any order and also in any groups of two?" I stop and look at her, hoping she'll nod yes.

She stares back. Then v-e-r-y s-l-o-w-l-y she begins to nod. "And it's the same for commutative?" she says.

"Yes! Yes!" I cheer. "It is! Go, Grace!"

She grins and gives me a high five. Then she wrinkles her forehead and chews on her thumbnail. "But I only barely get it."

"Barely's a start. Okay, math world, here we come!" I cheer. For the next hour and a half, we work at it. Gradually, Grace begins to do better.

While Grace works at the problems, I begin to feel restless. I get up and walk to the kitchen window. Then I notice the laminated photos on the refrigerator door. Grace's class pictures going back to kindergarten are placed in chronological order and held by identical magnets (not like the magnets on our refrigerator, which range from rubber bananas to cows to the happy teeth from our dentist). The thing that I hadn't noticed the first time I was at the house, but can't stop staring at now, is Grace's first-grade class picture. I was in the same class as Grace. My little face is right there. But the teacher we had is not the person in that picture. I keep trying to refocus my eyes to get it right. I move closer, then even closer, until my nose practically touches the photo. "Grace?" I say. "Where's Mrs. Joneska?"

"Hmmm?" she answers, not looking up.

"Mrs. Joneska, our first-grade teacher." I touch a raised part of the photo where the head is. Someone has carefully glued the head of someone else right over the place where Mrs. Joneska belongs. "Grace, what's with this picture?"

Grace finally looks up. "Oh. My mother had a fight with Mrs. Joneska, so she glued the head of a teacher she likes better on top."

I just stand there, not saying a word. Then I go back to the table and sit down. "That's unbelievable," I mumble.

"Yup," Grace agrees, looking back at the problems.

Twice I get up to call home, check on Cheddar, and say I'm not quite done yet. And twice Grace's mother gives us snacks. Rice crackers, carrot sticks, and sugar-free cocoa. She interrupts us less than the last time. Maybe she knows better than to mess with Grace at a time like this. You can't miss the tension.

At six-thirty, I push back my chair. "Okay, now I have to go. My mom's on her way over to pick me up."

"*Now?*" Grace asks. "You're leaving *now?*"

"I have to. My family's holding dinner for me, and I've got other homework to do. Don't worry, you'll—"

"But, Kat, you could eat here and then we could work longer."

"Grace, you're doing well with the problems we've gone over. You're not as bad at math as you think. Go through the review section again. You don't need me sitting here for that. If you get stuck, call. You'll be okay."

"Think so?" she asks, looking uncertain.

"Yeah, I do." I'm not sure if I really do or not. But eventually even Annie Sullivan and Professor Higgins had to call it a night.

☙

"What's the matter with *you?*" Hannah asks, when I drop my backpack on the floor with a dramatic thud.

"Tired," I answer, heading toward Cheddar's corner, where she waits, thumping her tail.

"Well, we're all starving, waiting for you. So don't dump attitude in here," Hannah says. She's wearing my silver hoop earrings.

"So don't keep snitching my stuff," I shoot back.

Dad looks at us. "Ahem. Ladies, let's be pleasant. Supper's on the table."

We just finish our dinner salad and potatoes stuffed with broccoli and melted cheese, when the phone rings. As soon as I pick up, I know by the hyperventilating sounds on the other end that it has to be Grace. "Relax," I urge. "Take a deep breath. No, you don't have amnesia. Give it a moment. It'll come back. Think. The axiom of reciprocals states . . . uh-huh . . . yup. Right, you got it! Yes, it has to be a non-zero number. Yup. Good." We both breathe a sigh of relief.

Grace babbles for a bit about her test preparation strategy. "My mother's giving me wheat germ for my brain. Couldn't hurt, right?"

Then she tells me she's decided to make an audiocassette tape of every definition, axiom, principle, property, equation, sample question, historical note and picture caption covered in chapters one, two, and three of our math book. She's going to sleep with the tape playing next to her ear. And her mom is going to get up during the night and rewind it so Grace can hear it over and over. I wonder what Annie Sullivan and Professor Higgins would think of that.

~✿~

It's late by the time I finish everything I have to do. Before I go to bed, I check on Cheddar. She seems stronger and more like herself. "Lookin' good, Cheddar. Dr. Goldstein did a great job. Maybe he's your fairy godfather." I kiss her good night.

I lie in bed thinking about the test tomorrow. Maybe there's a fairy godperson who could help Grace. A Magical Math Fairy Godperson, wearing a graduation cap and gown covered with equations, with glittery calculators in place of eyes, waving a silver metric stick that showers shiny numerals through the air. Boy, wouldn't the class freak out to see this image hovering over Grace, sprinkling her with math magic.

23

HOPING TO FIND A NEWLY MATH-
empowered Grace when I get to homeroom, I'm met at the door instead by a jittery, jumpy Grace. "Oh, my gosh. Oh, my gosh," she sputters, holding the sides of her head with her hands. "My head is full of math mush."

Math mush isn't exactly what I was hoping for, but I act calm. "Stay cool, and just reach into your brain's math file and pull out what you need for each question. You can do it. It's all in there." I hope I'm right.

While Mr. Billings is passing out the test papers, Grace wheezes, "Oh, my gosh. Here it comes. Oh, my gosh. Here it comes," over and over.

"Having a baby or what, Grace?" Keith says.

I turn around to speak to Grace. "Ignore that. Take your time and remember how you solved the problems last night. You know what you're doing. You'll be fine." I hope.

"Yeah, and try to estimate the answer before you work out the problem," Abby suggests. "That helps."

"Oooh, oooh, Mr. Billings, may I get a drink?" Grace asks. Then she whispers to me, "Got extra vitamins in my pocket. I'm taking them now and hoping they'll race up to my brain."

I laugh, but secretly loosen the laces of my sneakers to aid circulation and take out my hair clip so my brain won't feel pinched.

During the test, I can hear Grace mumbling and erasing behind me. Three times she gets up to ask Mr. Billings a question. Each time she walks back to her desk with a confused expression on her face.

Five minutes before the period ends, Mr. Billings says, "All right, time's up. Be sure your name and class section are on your papers. Pass them forward." When he has all the tests, Mr. Billings asks, "Well, how'd you do? Questions?"

Tim's hand goes up. "That second word problem about the rock band with the flat tire. Was '53 kilometers from Woodstock' the answer?"

Mr. Billings nods. Grace murmurs, "Uh-oh."

"And for that long equation at the end of page one," Abby asks, "was 47 the value of x?"

Another nod from Mr. Billings. Another "uh-oh" from Grace. So much for my Magical Math Fairy.

"Later today I have a study hall to monitor and then I have a prep period, so I should be able to get these tests corrected by the end of the day," Mr. Billings tells us as the bell rings.

"If any of you want to stop by my homeroom to get your grades, I'll be available."

Grace swallows so hard I can hear her. I stand up to leave, and put my hand on Grace's shoulder. She sits like a stone. "Time to go," I say.

"My mother's going to kill me," she murmurs.

"Grace, first of all, you don't know how you did. Not for sure, anyway. And second, you don't know that she'll be all that upset. Maybe she won't."

"Ohhh, yes, she will. Ohhh, yes, yes, yes." Grace's head bobs up and down.

I remember what happened to Mrs. Joneska's head and wonder if Grace's will be next. "Come on," I urge. "I'll go with you after eighth period to get the results."

Abby stands by the door waiting. "Grace, a lot of kids thought it was hard. And it was. You're not the only one who missed some answers."

Grace just shakes her head and walks like a zombie. "I won't even get points for neatness. I erased holes through my papers."

I stop at my locker. "See you later in social studies, Grace. Try not to worry."

〜⌾〜

Dennis Boyle is standing in the doorway of Mr. Corento's room when I get to science. As I start to pass by, he turns sideways so that his backpack knocks me into the doorjamb. "Oh! Ex-cuuuuse me," Dennis says, trying to act surprised.

"What is your problem, Dennis?" I glare at him, dreading another scene.

He glares back. All at once I am seeing not just this tall seventh-grade boy who's beginning to get a mustache, but also a smaller Dennis, riding his bike back and forth in front of my house tormenting me. "Dennis, is this really about Melody's bike? Or is it about something from a while ago?"

"What are you talking about?" He pushes his hair back, then fiddles with the metal clip hanging from his belt loop.

"The summer before sixth grade."

He lets out a puff of air. "Get serious. I don't know what you mean."

"A pool party Keith had. You wanted me to go with you. I said no. You were mad. But I told you that my parents didn't think it was appropriate to have a date for the party." Putting some of it on my folks is okay, since they actually did think that. Dennis doesn't have to know I wasn't any more likely to go out with him back then than I am now.

He just stands there. His face is red. Kids squeeze by to get to their seats. I speak in a low voice. "Look Dennis, I don't mean to embarrass you. I'd appreciate it if you'd stop making me out to be a criminal. And anyway, you already got back at me by calling me 'bird-brain, turd-brain.'"

Dennis smirks. "Don't flatter yourself, freckle-face, and get a fat head thinking some stupid little thing you did over a year ago matters to me." He starts toward his desk, then turns. "Sorry about your dog getting hurt, though."

That last remark surprised me. But then this is my year for surprises.

There is no pranking or fooling around during science. Mrs. Eliaz walks in and sits in the back of the room. I wonder if she is there to observe the class, an uneasy-looking Mr. Corento, or me. But after a while, I forget she's there and begin wondering about Dennis. Would the talk we had get him off my back or just make things worse?

Outside Mr. Billings's room at the end of the day, there's a lot of nervous talk about the test. "What about that word problem about the hamburgers, cheeseburgers, and tofuburgers?" Keith asks. "I didn't have a clue, I just got hungry."

"Yeah, and that one about the levels of caffeine in drinks," Matthew says. "I guessed."

"See, Grace?" I point out. "Lots of people didn't do so hot."

Mr. Billings calls us in. "Hi kids, bus call starts in seven minutes, so we won't be able to go over the test. Tomorrow in class we'll do that. But I know you'd like to find out how you did." He pulls a stack of papers out of his desk drawer. "I'm announcing now that I'll be starting an after-school help group twice a week. Some of you will want to come to that."

"I guess that means scores weren't so good, huh?" Keith says, cracking his knuckles.

"About what I expected for the first test in a tough course. Some excellent, some good, and some not so terrific," Mr. Billings answers. "But we're only a few weeks into the marking period. We can do something about the trouble some of you are having. Anyone with a C or lower should plan to attend the help group."

He begins to hand out papers. I can pretty much tell what grades kids get by the expressions on their faces. And some of the kids I've known so long I can predict their grades. Abby, Tim, and Matthew all get B+'s. Keith gets a C+. Grace stands frozen, holding, her C–. I don't know if she notices that there are a couple of D's.

The bus calls begin over the loudspeakers. "Time to go, Grace," I say.

"You got an A, didn't you?" she asks, not moving.

"Minus."

"Okay, minus. You're so lucky, Kat—" she begins, but Mr. Billings interrupts.

"Grace, the work you showed with the problems was good. You were really close to solving each of the problems you missed. Perhaps you panicked. But we'll work together to clear up whatever confusion you're having." His voice is friendly and he doesn't sound like a teacher who is about to drop a student to a lower class.

"You think I'll be able to do this math?" Grace asks. "I mean, if I work hard and come to the after-school help group, you think I'll survive this class?"

Mr. Billings laughs. "Yes, I do. I want my students to succeed. I'm like a dog with a bone on that. I don't give up. My teaching style and your learning style may take time to get in sync. But we'll get there."

Grace finally exhales all that air she sucked out of the room yesterday. "You think?"

"Yup. I think," he answers.

We leave Mr. Billings's room and go to our lockers. Grace looks like a different person from the one who dragged out of math class that morning. "That wasn't so bad. You doing okay now?" I ask.

"Yes. And Kat, thank you."

"I'm glad I was able to help you, at least some." I close my locker and pick up my backpack.

"No, really, Kat. Thank you."

"You're welcome." I wave at Grace and head home.

24

THE BIG D HOVERS, GHOSTLIKE.
I see it as a huge white D-shaped blimp, decorated with dollar signs and tethered with a rope to my ankle; I want to shrink it out of existence. Until it's gone, I can't enjoy what would normally be free time because I know I need to be earning money. I'm learning more about my neighbors' lawns, pets, and children than I ever thought I'd know. But bit by bit, the debt is deflating.

My afternoons with Mrs. Lawrence continue. Mr. Lawrence has asked me to help out a couple of extra times, in addition to when his men's club meets. On Columbus Day, I'm off from school, so Mr. Lawrence is able to plan some additional time for himself. I arrive after lunch and find Mrs. Lawrence at the kitchen table looking through pictures. "Ann has a drawer of photographs that could use organizing, Kat," Mr. Lawrence says. "I don't have albums for them right now, but perhaps you two could group them. I have some shirt boxes that would work quite well for the time being."

When Mrs. Lawrence notices her husband getting ready to leave, she stands up and begins to follow him. "Are we going out now?" she asks.

Quickly I hold up a photograph of her and say, "What a nice outfit, Mrs. Lawrence." She looks at the photo, then at Mr. Lawrence, and begins to wring her hands. "The dress you are wearing here is right back in style again," I point out. "Look at that pattern and hem length."

Once he is out of sight, she relaxes. We talk about the pictures, and I learn not to ask too many questions. The old photos from a long time ago don't seem to cause problems, but the more recent ones do, and she gets frustrated when she can't recognize who is in them or where they were taken. There are dates on the backs of most of them, which helps with the organizing.

"My father always wore that hat fishing," Mrs. Lawrence says, smiling as she points to a picture of Mr. Lawrence who's wearing the same floppy hat I hooked when we went fishing. Maybe Mr. Lawrence inherited his father-in-law's fishing hat.

"Look at my father's chin. My brother has the same one," she says.

I nod, smiling at her, but I feel like crying. She can't separate her father from her husband. And is there even a brother, or is she confused about that, too? Maybe she means her son.

I want to straighten her mind, not just her photographs. Instead, I swallow hard and say, "Would you like me to make us some tea?"

"Why, that would be lovely, dear." She continues to pick up and examine photographs.

I serve the tea as nicely as I can, tea-party style, using china cups and saucers with a matching cream and sugar set. I make toast, sprinkle it with cinnamon, and cut it into little triangles.

We sip our tea and nibble our toast while Mrs. Lawrence holds up pictures and tells me about her family, her pets, her school days, her friends, and her vacations. And when she is confused, I change the subject by picking up a photo I think she'll be all right with.

We aren't quite finished sorting them when Mr. Lawrence comes home. He brings the mail, and shows Mrs. Lawrence a letter from an inn on Cape Cod. It confirms reservations. "We go every year," he explains to me. "We'll leave on Wednesday and plan to be away for a week, counting stops up and back to visit family."

"That sounds nice. When would you like me to be here next?" I ask.

Mr. Lawrence looks at the calendar on the wall. "Well, let's see. You'll be here tomorrow while I have my men's club meeting. And then there's the trip. So, it looks like after that, we'll see you again the Tuesday before Halloween."

Riding home on my bicycle, I think about what it might be like for Mrs. Lawrence to stay somewhere besides her own house; she might get really confused. I hope she'll be able to have some fun. And I hope she'll remember me when she gets home.

On Tuesday afternoon, Mrs. Lawrence and I finish sorting the photographs. As we close the last box, I reach in my shirt pocket and pull out a picture of me taken at the end of the summer when we were in Boston. "Here, Mrs. Lawrence. This is for you."

She takes the picture and studies it. Then she looks at me and smiles. "Thank you, dear." Picking up first one box, and another, looking at the dates we've written on the lids, she asks, "Where does this one belong?"

"Oh, you don't have to put it in a box, not yet anyway. It's a new picture of me. I thought you might like having it." Suddenly I feel foolish. What I did might only end up confusing her, because my picture and I belong in the category of recent, and that's what she's most mixed up about.

"Well, thank you," she says, propping it up on the shelf near the table. "It's very nice."

We water the indoor plants. "How about the flowers outside, Mrs. Lawrence? It might be good to water those, too." We unwind the hose and start around the yard with it. I'm careful not to leave her alone, not even for a minute to turn off the water. We do everything together, side by side.

Over our heads we hear the honking of Canada geese. They fly over us, the fanlike beating of their wings making the air pulse. We watch them landing in the river near the house. Ten, fifteen, twenty, thirty, fifty of them glide in and splash down. Mrs. Lawrence smiles as she watches the geese. "Another season, dear. Another season." I put my arm through hers as we stand there, and I wonder how she will be next year when the geese return.

Mr. Lawrence pulls in the driveway as we are coiling the hose and putting it away. "Hello, ladies. I hope you had a nice afternoon. My meeting was very interesting. The speaker was someone I went to school with years ago. Ann, you remember my high school friend named Artie McDodd, don't you?"

She does. Artie McDodd from sixty years ago is probably more clear to her than I am. And he doesn't have to give her a photograph of himself to help things along.

I give each of them a hug as I'm leaving and wish them a happy trip. They stand in the driveway together waving. I miss them already.

25

HUMMM . . . *MMM* . . . *MMM* . . .
There's always a hum right before the loudspeaker blares a school announcement. The way this school year has started, I've become hum-jumpy. People in high places, and some in low, still don't know whether I might be stealing and cannibalizing bicycles. I could be called to the office and questioned again any time.

Friday's first hum comes when Mr. Johnson, the custodian, is called to bring a mop and pail to the gym. I try not to think what he may have to clean up. The next hum comes before an announcement that lunch detention will be held in the Library Media Center. And the third hum signals a student being called to the office. I'm relieved not to hear my name.

After fourth period, I meet Grace on her way to her locker. "How's everything going, Grace?"

"Lots better, thanks. I have after-school math with Mr. Billings today. You were right about him, Kat. He's good at explaining and he's fun." She leans toward me and whispers in my ear, "And he's so-o-o cute. But don't tell anyone I said that." She grins and heads down the hall to her locker. "See you later."

I turn and crash right into Dennis.

"Watch yourself, bike klepto," he mutters.

I stare at his angry face. And then my gaze shifts to his belt clip. I realize that his chain is gone and, all at once, I know where I've seen it. It was caught on one of the bikes that the police pulled from the river.

"Dennis," I say slowly, "you're blaming me, but *you* took those bikes."

"You're crazy, turd-brain." He fingers his belt clip.

"Where's your chain?" I ask, looking him right in the eye.

Dennis looks at me blankly and shrugs.

"Well, *I* know where it is. It's with the police."

Dennis's face twists and turns red. "What the—"

"You left a big clue with those junked bikes, Dennis."

"Shut up, idiot," he answers.

"We both know who the bike klepto is, Dennis." I'm amazingly calm as I say that.

"I said *shut up!* You know *nothing!*" He spins and walks quickly down the hall.

I'm left standing there. Now the shaking starts. So much for big, brave me. I'm not sure what to do next. Tell maybe. What'll happen then? Slowly I turn toward my fifth-period class.

～இ～

In the lunchroom I walk mechanically to my table. Matthew drops his backpack on a seat. "Hmmm. Smells like Yankee Stadium in here. Save this place. I'm getting in line."

"You're actually going to *eat* a hot dog?" Abby asks. "Don't you know what's *in* them?"

"Yup," Matthew answers. "That's what makes them so good." He hurries off to get in line.

Abby looks at me. "You feel okay?"

I don't want to talk about what happened with Dennis yet. I have to think and figure out what to do next. I answer with, "I might be getting a cold or something."

Abby accepts my explanation and the boys don't notice I'm in a fog. Lunch ends and I get my books for my afternoon classes. Concentrating on anything except Dennis and what to do about him is impossible.

It's during last period that I hear the hum. Then it comes. *"Katia Randall to the office. Katia Randall to the office."*

"Oh, no," I whisper. "Not again." My heart begins to pound and my face turns red. With everyone staring at me, I walk out of class and to the office.

Mrs. Landes points toward Mrs. Eliaz's door. "Katia, Mrs. Eliaz would like to speak with you."

I knock on the door, which Mrs. Eliaz opens. "Hello, Katia. Come in."

The next person I see is my father. He stands up and puts his arm around my shoulder. "It's okay, Kat. Don't be upset. Here, sit down." He points to the wooden chair next to him.

Slouched in a corner chair is Dennis Boyle. On one side of him is Lieutenant Scott. On the other side is a woman dressed in a jogging suit. Dennis glances up at me, then looks down at his lap.

I rub my sweaty palms on my shaking knees, and my mind races as I try to figure out what's going on. The police must know about Dennis. Did Dennis turn himself in? Did some-one else?

"Katia," Mrs. Eliaz says, "you know Dennis. This is Mrs. Boyle, and we also have Lieutenant Scott with us. We would like to talk with you about the matter of Melody Whiezersky's bicycle. I know you have told your story before, but it would be helpful if you would clarify some details." She leans forward in her seat, turning toward Dennis and his mother. "Mrs. Boyle, I'm going to ask that you and Dennis take a seat in the outside office area for a few minutes while we speak with Katia."

When the door shuts behind them, Lieutenant Scott says, "Miss Randall, we'd like to ask you some questions concern-ing the disappearance of the Whiezersky bicycle."

My throat is suddenly dry. I swallow twice.

They ask why I took the bike from the school bike rack. They ask if it was the only bike I ever took. Lieutenant Scott scribbles notes on what looks like the same police report I saw before.

"So you never saw the bicycle after you left it outside the animal hospital?" Mrs. Eliaz asks.

"No," I answer. "Not until it was pulled out of the river. Lieutenant Scott and Sergeant Tiani were there when that happened."

"At what time did you discover the bicycle gone?" Lieutenant Scott continues.

I think back to that afternoon. "It was about three-thirty. I remember looking at the clock around the time I left. And when I called my house, my sister was already there. She takes the bus from the high school."

"Okay, approximately three-thirty," Lieutenant Scott says, writing it down. He raises his head, looking directly at me. "And please explain why you were there on that bridge the day the bike was found."

"Because I had been on Frogtown Road, helping Mr. Lawrence by looking after Mrs. Lawrence. She can't ever stay alone. I was riding home. That's the way I go."

"All right. Thank you, Katia," Mrs. Eliaz says. "Lieutenant Scott, do you have any further questions for Katia?"

He shakes his head. "Now I'd like to speak with Dennis again."

"Dennis tells quite a different story, Katia," Mrs. Eliaz states. "And we're trying to get to the truth." She stands up. "Mr. Randall and Katia, if you don't mind, please take a seat outside. We will want to talk with you some more."

For a second time, I walk out of that office stunned and confused. Mrs. Eliaz calls Dennis and his mother back inside and the door shuts.

I'm still shaking when Dad and I sit down on the folding chairs outside Mrs. Eliaz's office. "Dad, what do the police know?"

Dad shakes his head and takes my hand. "I'm not certain, Kat. Whatever's going on is serious, but I'm positive this has much more to do with Dennis than with you."

"Then why'd you get called to be here?" I ask.

"School policy. When the police come in to question a student, parents are supposed to be present. Everything's going to be all right. Relax. Take some deep breaths," he says, getting up. "I'm going to go find a water fountain and a men's room. Be back in a minute." He's out the door before I can tell him about the chain.

I rub my temples and lean my head back against the wall. Suddenly I realize that I can hear people speaking on the other side of the wall.

"Okay, Dennis," Lieutenant Scott begins, "where did you say you were after school on September sixth?"

I hear Dennis mumble something like, "Don't remember."

"Mrs. Boyle? Do you remember?" Mrs. Eliaz asks.

Mrs. Boyle clears her throat. "Well, that would have been the first day of school, right? Hmmm . . . I don't recall, not specifically. Dennis usually goes off with his older brother in the afternoons. I suppose that's where he was."

"Where do you boys go?" Mrs. Eliaz asks Dennis.

"Hang out," Dennis answers.

"Would that be near the veterinary hospital?" Lieutenant Scott asks.

I hear my breath catch.

There's no answer right away. Lieutenant Scott repeats the question louder.

"Uhhhh, we just hang out. No place special," Dennis replies.

Dad returns at the same time that three sixth-grade girls walk into the office and start talking to Mrs. Landes. I can't clearly hear what's going on behind the wall anymore. The girls explain that they were sent from social studies class to read about Christopher Columbus over the loudspeaker. Mrs. Landes replies, "I was warned, or rather I was informed, earlier of your commemorative readings." She introduces the Columbus Day readers over the intercom and then hands them the microphone. Each girl reads from a separate sheet of paper. With stops for unpracticed, hard-to-pronounce words and for giggling, it takes a while for them to finish.

Finally it's quiet enough to hear Mrs. Boyle talking inside Mrs. Eliaz's office. "Dennis, how can you sit there and say that? They were found right in our shed."

Dad and I look at each other.

"We'll need to see both boys down at police headquarters later today," Lieutenant Scott says.

"Dennis, as of right now, you are suspended. Get your things out of your locker," Mrs. Eliaz directs, "and wait outside this office. We'll be done shortly."

The door opens abruptly and bangs back against something. Maybe Mrs. Eliaz's desk. Dennis walks out and the door shuts behind him. Not caring who hears, Dennis mutters, "*Busted*. Satisfied, turd-brain?" as he leaves the office.

"That's one angry kid," Dad says.

"Dad, I just figured out a short while ago that Dennis took the bikes, but I didn't even tell anyone yet. So, I don't get it."

The door opens again. As Mrs. Boyle walks out, I hear Lieutenant Scott say, "I'll see you, with Mr. Boyle and both boys, at the station at five o'clock."

Mrs. Boyle nods. She turns to me. "Dennis owes you an apology. And another one to Melody Whiezersky. I'm sorry, Kat. And I'm sorry, Mr. Randall." She sighs and walks to the office door to wait for Dennis to return.

Lieutenant Scott leans out of the doorway and gestures for us to come back into Mrs. Eliaz's office.

Mrs. Eliaz points toward the chairs. "Thank you both for your patience. We were finally able to get to the truth." She explains that a student came to the office with information that was helpful. Dennis and his brother have been caught with stolen bike parts. Pieces of Melody's bike were among those found in a shed behind the Boyles' house.

Dennis claimed he didn't know anything about the parts. Even though his story wasn't believable, Mrs. Eliaz and Lieutenant Scott wanted to hear my story again. Finally, Dennis admitted what's been going on.

"What about the other Boyle boy? Where is he?" Dad asks.

"At the high school," Lieutenant Scott answers. "Sergeant Tiani is handling that end of it."

I listen, still amazed that Dennis has done something so awful. And just when I'm starting to wonder when someone is going to offer me a very big, heartfelt apology, Lieutenant Scott says, "You've been through a lot, Miss Randall, but you must understand that you are not entirely guiltless. You did, technically, take a bike. We know why you did it, but that does not erase the fact that you took another person's property without permission. Because of the unusual circumstances, and because the Whiezerskys have their replacement bike, the matter will be dropped."

"It is unfortunate that you had to be questioned about further bike thefts, Katia," Mrs. Eliaz says, "but when you do something impetuous such as you did, you must anticipate unpleasant consequences. And Katia," Mrs. Eliaz continues, "we expect that nothing like that type of borrowing will occur again. Correct?"

"Yes. Correct." I guess that's as close as I'm going to get to an apology.

Dad clears his throat. "Kat has felt the burden of her mistake since the moment the bike disappeared from the veterinary hospital. I'm sure nothing like it will ever happen again."

Lieutenant Scott adds, "I'm sure, too." And then he actually smiles at me.

Dad and I say good-bye at the office door. "Dad, I'm so sorry about all this. It must have been embarrassing having to come here today."

"Not so bad. Besides, we wouldn't want life to get dull." He winks at me. "And now, your reputation is on its way up. That's important. Want a ride home?"

"No thanks. I want to see a few friends." I watch Dad walk to the front door and then I go to my locker. The end-of-school bell rings and Abby, Matthew, and Tim hurry to meet me and hear what happened. Abby is outraged at what I've been through. "*What?* No apology?" She waves her finger wildly. "That's appalling!"

"Yeah," I agree, "I was expecting a big-time *I'm sorry.*"

Tim nods. "Yeah. You should have gotten one. And what a sleazeball Dennis is to try and pin his crime on you."

Matthew agrees. "Total scuzzball."

Abby puts her arm on my shoulder. "We'll help resurrect your reputation, Kat."

I wonder if news about me *not* being in trouble will spread as fast as the news that I was. Probably not.

I mention that some student gave the office information about Dennis. None of us can figure out who that was.

"So, what happens to Dennis now?" Tim asks. "I mean, he's kind of young for jail."

"It's not the first time those brothers have gotten into trouble," Matthew answers. "So I think Dennis might have to go to juvenile court and maybe to a juvenile detention center. For his brother, it'll probably be worse."

"Wow," Abby murmurs.

"It's scary what kind of trouble Dennis and his brother are in," I say. "It's hard not to feel somewhat sorry—"

"Jeez, Kat. They brought it on themselves," Matthew says.

Buses are being called and the hallways are clearing as we walk toward the front door. "What a horrendous day," I say.

"You've lived through more drama in a few weeks than most people have in a few years," Abby says.

"What's with you, huh? Allergic to calm?" Tim asks.

"Not exactly." I shrug. "Things just happen."

"Fat understatement," Matthew remarks.

"You need to do something relaxing now, Kat," Abby suggests. "Like fishing."

I nod. "Yeah, good idea. Maybe Saturday."

The boys stop short and stare at us. *"Fishing?"* they say in unison.

"You joking?" Tim asks.

"No, why?" Abby answers, defensively. "I happen to like fishing. And Kat does, too."

I don't mention that I'm as likely to catch a hat as a fish.

The boys look stunned. "You seriously like fishing?" Tim asks.

"Yup," Abby answers. "I've fished practically my whole life."

Tim's eyes light up. "Me, too. So, let's all go on Saturday."

Abby is glowing. You'd think we were going to the palace ball.

❧

I'm crossing the road in front of the school, when I hear Grace calling after me, "Hey Kat!" She waits for a car to pass, then hurries to where I'm standing. "Well, you must be feeling better, I bet." She has an odd look on her face.

I nod. "Yeah. Much."

"The chain, huh?" Grace smiles.

My mouth opens wide. She knows. How does she know?

"I've *never* been able to mind my own business, you know. And when I was down the hall at my locker, I heard Dennis and you talking about that chain. Well, what's a friend to do? Huh?"

I have to laugh. The self-appointed seventh-grade snitch strikes again. The first time she meddled, I wanted to wring her neck. This time I want to hug her.

～⊙～

It's a crisp, bright afternoon and the leaves are turning colors. I take Cheddar into the backyard when I get home. I sit on the steps watching her. She's moving more easily now, putting some weight on the injured leg. Monday she'll visit Dr. Goldstein. Her leg will be checked, and her grubby cast will be replaced with a new one.

Dad has made the backyard fence more Cheddar-proof. Right now she's more interested in snacking than in attempting another breakout. She's in the corner of the yard where the fall raspberry crop grows and she's gingerly pulling some of the last berries off the canes. She has her own distinct berry-picking style. She puts her lips around a berry and then she backs up until it pops off in her mouth.

A monarch butterfly clings to a raspberry cane. I want to think it's my river monarch, juicing up before its long migration. It must be one of the last to leave.

When Cheddar and I go inside, Dad shows me a note that we've just gotten from Dr. Goldstein. He wrote to tell us that Mr. Lawrence has not only paid the expenses of Cheddar's treatment, but he has also made a large donation to the animal hospital to help with costs of treating other injured pets.

I get a chunk of cheese from the refrigerator and settle down on the floor next to Cheddar. She gives me her crooked smile. It feels so good to be sharing a piece of cheese with my dog. *Thump, thump.* I think about the Lawrences on their trip and hope that Mrs. Lawrence is all right. "Cheddar, how would you like to come with me to visit the Lawrences, when your leg is better?" *Thump.*

Hannah strolls into the kitchen looking for a snack. "Hey, Kat. Sounds like things are looking up." She takes an apple. "See, I told you this would be one of your best years." She gives a wave and heads back upstairs.

"Hannah?" I call.

"Yeah?"

"Nice earrings!"

Thump.